CEOS DON'T CRY

CEOS DON'T CRY

•

Joselyn Vaughn

AVALON BOOKS
NEW YORK

Published by Thomas Bouregy & Co., Inc.
160 Madison Avenue, New York, NY 10016

Library of Congress Cataloging-in-Publication Data

Vaughn, Joselyn.
CEOs don't cry / Joselyn Vaughn.
    p. cm.
ISBN 978-0-8034-9945-4 (hardcover : acid-free paper)
I. Title.

PS3622.A953C46 2009
813'.6—dc22

                                        2008048214

PRINTED IN THE UNITED STATES OF AMERICA
ON ACID-FREE PAPER
BY HADDON CRAFTSMEN, BLOOMSBURG, PENNSYLVANIA

263 p.

For Joe, thanks for all your encouragement.
Special thanks to Wendy for getting me this far.

Chapter One

"Could this day get any worse?" Leslie Knotts muttered to herself, eyeing the watermark-circled hole in the ceiling tiles above her head. Thudding and a muffled expletive rumbled from the hole.

She yanked her cashmere scarf from her neck and stomped the slush off of her Prada heels. She took one look around her new office in the Carterville branch of Hanston and Boyd Accounting and gasped. This place was a mere phone call away from being condemned.

Someone had shoved the room's few pieces of furniture haphazardly to one side in favor of a paint-spattered ladder, and water stains marked the paneling and the worn carpet.

As the jingling of the bells on the door died away, something scraped against the ceiling above her, and dust sifted onto her hair. Leslie snatched the handle of her Coach briefcase and backed into the door, jangling

1

the sleigh bells on the knob again. If a rodent appeared in the hole, she would drive all the way back to Chicago tonight. She forced herself to take a deep breath, murmuring hopefully that rats didn't swear.

"Just a minute!" shouted a deep voice from the ceiling, just before a boot crashed through a stained tile, sending soggy chunks of it raining down onto Leslie's head. "Crap."

"What in the world?" she hissed, flicking a hunk of tile off her shoulder. This Podunk place probably didn't even have a decent dry cleaner, she thought, eyeing the wet spots on her suit.

Two booted feet slid out of the hole, followed by worn, dusty jeans, a T-shirt, and two muscular arms. Leslie's fingers relaxed around her briefcase. She wouldn't mind seeing that descend from her own ceiling on occasion.

"Hi," the man said as he balanced on the ladder, then climbed down. He tossed a flashlight into an open toolbox. Then he looked at her with bright blue eyes, his hair littered with cobwebs.

Watching him descend the ladder was the best part of her day. Not that getting transferred here and spending four hours driving on snowy roads constituted a stellar one. His jeans and T-shirt clung in just the right places, and she couldn't help but smile back at the grin on his face.

"Problems up there?" she asked, heat rising in her cheeks. She didn't see men like this in the city very often.

"Did Minnie send you? Or Yvonne?" he asked, his gaze traveling over her body. He pursed his lips, and she thought he was annoyed about something.

"Who?" she asked, self-consciously checking her hair for clumps of ceiling tile. "No, Chuck did. I'm the new manager, Leslie Knotts. I didn't mean to interrupt your work. I was expecting a receptionist, not a handyman."

A look of relief crossed his face. He wiped his hands across his backside and held one out to her. She shook it, shocked by its roughness. There was something headily masculine about it. He didn't spend all his time at a keyboard.

"Mark Schultz. A pipe burst up there two weeks ago. We shut off the water, but something's still dripping. I got tired of tripping over buckets, so I climbed up there to check it out."

"Two weeks? Why wasn't it fixed before?" She stepped over the remnants of the ceiling tile and peered up into the gap. The hole was directly over the one unfaded spot of carpet where the receptionist's desk had been.

"No one to authorize it, since Mr. Perkins retired." He kicked a piece of rubbish aside. "Roof's leaking, too. Which explains the water stains on the wall. This place is falling apart."

"Another thing to add to my list," Leslie mumbled—*of reasons to add Tabasco to Chuck's coffee,* she added to herself. "Where's the receptionist? They told me there'd be one." She leaned to look down a narrow hallway stretching away from the reception area.

"Mr. Perkins hired me part-time right before Christmas. Then he retired a week later, which conveniently coincided with the pipes bursting and left me with nothing to do until the new branch manager arrived. Would you like some coffee? I think the pot's still warm."

He was her receptionist? Part-time, at least. This was like one of Chuck's fantasies, except her receptionist was male. Chuck definitely preferred a sexy female receptionist. Now she had a sexy male one. Chuck's fantasy had included five females. He'd told her about it during coffee breaks when he picked her brain for ideas so he could steal her promotion.

"No thanks. There's more water damage?" she asked, reminding herself to focus on the situation at hand. Turning this dump around was going to take all her energy. If it was possible at all. Chuck must have laughed himself silly after she left this morning. He'd known the exact condition of the place.

"Unfortunately, yes. It's an old building, and with this cold weather and the lack of insulation, the pipes have been freezing and cracking. Most of it's in here. There's more by the rear entrance. I haven't investigated yet, but it didn't seem as urgent as this."

"Have you done repair work like this before?" she asked, eyeing the tools hooked to his belt and the way his jeans clung to his hips.

"Here and there. Mostly for my aunt. She's always got me fixing things for her." He shrugged. "It's been quiet here all day. I figured I could work on the repairs without disturbing anyone."

"Given the sales reports I glanced at this morning, I doubt anyone will disturb us until April twelfth. We'll be madly busy for three days, and then we can close until next year." She rolled her eyes. She'd be using her CPA to file 1040 EZ forms.

He glanced around the office and shoved some of the buckets aside with his foot. "Sorry it's such a mess. I didn't expect you until tomorrow morning. I thought I'd have more of this cleaned up by then. Normally, I wear a tie, but . . ." He gestured to the ceiling. "Minnie's always harping on me about wearing my good clothes when I work on projects like this."

"Minnie?"

"My aunt. Avoid her if you can. She's got some crazy hobbies."

Leslie inwardly sighed in relief. Not a wife or girl-friend. Not that it mattered. She cleared her throat. "I arrived in town earlier than I expected and thought I should stop in and see the place. Maybe get a head start on preparations for the upcoming tax season. Making lists. You know, dive right in." She laughed uncomfortably. She sounded like a workaholic. Not that there was anything wrong with liking your job. Would the effort be worth it here? Working here wouldn't get her a partnership, that was for sure.

"I can give you the dime tour." Mark tilted his head toward the hallway. "It's not worth much more."

Leslie nodded. Realizing she still clutched her briefcase in front of her like a girl on her first day of school, she leaned it against the desk and hung her coat and scarf on the coat tree beside the door.

"That's my desk." He gestured to the iron gray desk adorned with only an empty wire basket and a stapler. "Your office is through here." Mark tapped a glass door with two fingers and pointed down the hall. Two doors on the opposite side of the hallway led to bathrooms. "Mr. Perkins turned the women's bathroom into storage and used the men's."

Leslie grimaced. "There can't be that much need for storage. We store everything on the servers now. We don't need paper backups."

"We can change things back. Mr. Perkins liked paper."

"I see. What's through here?" She gestured toward a frosted glass door at the end of the hallway.

"That's the break room. There's a refrigerator, micro-wave, coffeepot—all that good stuff."

Mark opened the door to the manager's office. Leslie brushed past him to glance through the doorway. Piles of papers and boxes were stacked on the desk, cascading out of cabinet drawers, and sliding off chairs throughout the office. Lots of papers but no computer. A fax ma-chine with its receiving tray filled with paper stood on a portable cart. The only color in the room besides that of aged paper was provided by a row of troll snow-globes on the front edge of the desk.

"I would've tried to file this stuff or something, but short of setting fire to the whole mess, I didn't know where to start." Mark crossed his arms and leaned against the doorjamb.

"I was having the same thought. About setting fire to it, that is." Leslie stepped into the room and poked at some of the piles. She tugged open one of the file cabi-net drawers and found it stuffed with more paper. "I don't understand why there's so much paper here. The sales reports didn't show this much activity. Maybe last year was a bad year." She turned back to the desk. "Where are the computers? He should have at least one to electronically file tax returns. I didn't see one in the reception area either."

Mark hefted a box of files and uncovered a computer resting on the floor next to one of the filing cabinets. "There's this one. I never saw Mr. Perkins use it, though. The one on my desk got fried when the pipe burst. I had a friend look at it, but it's dead. He's trying to extract some files from the hard drive, but he wasn't optimistic. I hope there are backups somewhere."

One computer and, given the yellowing of the plastic case, an old one. Leslie rolled her eyes. Why hadn't this Perkins guy requisitioned new ones when the company upgraded their systems last year? Being a partner's godfather obviously allowed him to shirk several corporate demands. At least she had her laptop with all the current software. He didn't even have high-speed Internet access. She mentally added that to her list. How had he done any electronic filing? No wonder this branch hadn't recorded a profit in almost a decade.

"I've got my work cut out for me," she mumbled. "I should tear the place down and start over."

Mark grabbed the papers out of the fax machine and handed them to her. "Maybe you can make sense out of these. They've been coming in all day. I know Mr. Perkins didn't use e-mail, so headquarters faxed a lot of stuff."

He shoved some papers on the desk aside and found a set of keys. He quickly flipped through them and then handed the set to her, holding one key up. "This one's for the front door. The door's warped, so it's hard to lock. You have to lean against it and then turn the key."

"Thanks." She dropped the keys into her pocket. "What's with the trolls?"

Mark picked up one of the snow-globes on the desk and shook it. "Mr. Perkins' grandkids gave them to him, I guess. I don't know why he didn't take them. Kinda creepy, if you ask me." He put the globe back on the desk and shook his head.

Leslie smiled uncomfortably at him. What should she do now? He looked as if he was waiting for her instructions. She was supposed to be the manager; she was supposed to know these things.

"I'm going to look these over for a few minutes," she said, waving the faxes. "Then I'll find my hotel room. What do you need to finish on the pipes?"

"Not much. I'll pick up a replacement pipe at the hardware store tomorrow morning, and then I'll finish the repair." He leaned against the door frame. "I'll have the mess cleaned up by tomorrow afternoon. Where are you staying?"

Leslie reached into her purse for the crumpled printout of directions from the Internet. "The Lilac Bower on Oak Street. It was the only listing I could find with long-term rentals. I hope it's not a dive."

"My aunt, Minnie, owns it. I guess you can't avoid her." He shoved his hands into his pockets. "The rooms are nice. You won't have to worry about that."

"Oh." Leslie felt her face flush with heat. "I'm sorry. I didn't mean to imply—"

Mark shook his head. "No worries. It's exactly as the name sounds." He coughed. "Purple."

Leslie's lips twitched, and her gaze locked with

Mark's. Merriment filled his eyes, and Leslie felt something strange happen inside her. She started to laugh. At the sound of Mark's low chuckle, Leslie's heart flipped over. Her fingers released the faxed papers, and they scattered to the floor.

"Let me get those." Mark knelt and shuffled the papers together.

Leslie's gaze followed his hands. His fingers looked scuffed, and a purple bruise marred his thumbnail. A shiver traveled down her spine at the thought that he'd smashed it with a hammer.

"Thanks." She snatched the papers from him and hurried toward the door. "I'll see you tomorrow," she said while whipping her scarf around her neck and throwing her jacket over her arm.

"Hey, if Minnie invites you to the library, don't go!" he called after her as the bells on the doorknob jangled.

Mark scanned the shelves before pulling out two woodworking books. He flipped to the table of contents to see what projects were included. He saw an Arts and Crafts chair he wanted to make, so he tucked the book under his arm.

He had come to the library to find books on organizing his business records and preparing the reports he needed for his taxes, but the remodeling and woodworking books caught his attention, as they always did. He forced himself to walk farther down the aisle until he stood in front of the business section. Titles like *Starting Your Own Business* and *Your First Business Plan* glared at him. He reluctantly pulled them off the shelf and flipped through them, not really looking at the pages. He hated reading this stuff. Marketing plans and double-entry accounting never made any sense to him.

Groaning, he shoved the business-plan book back onto the shelf. He didn't need a plan for starting a business; he needed something on how to organize the pile of crumpled receipts he'd stuffed into a manila envelope. He scratched his head and bent to the bottom shelf, examining the books there. They didn't look any more promising than those on the previous shelf.

He should hire someone to do it for him or at least get some kind of bookkeeping system arranged for him. Unfortunately, that meant cash, and he didn't have a lot on hand.

When he'd started filling in at Hanston and Boyd, he hoped to learn some of the ins and outs of keeping a business organized. Mr. Perkins had said they might hire more tax preparers as the tax season started. But he'd never placed an ad in the paper or put a HELP WANTED sign in the window. So far there hadn't been enough business to warrant it. Mark had answered only a handful of phone calls since he started at the accounting firm. He figured the activity must pick up after the holidays. But then Mr. Perkins abruptly retired on Christmas Eve, and Mark had been stuck there for the last week by himself.

Leslie, the new manager, looked as if she would rather chew glass shards than be here. If he had any money, he'd bet this transfer wasn't what she'd been gunning for. He'd guess she'd been aiming higher on the corporate ladder.

It was too bad, really, that she seemed so uptight. French twists and slim figures weren't his type, but if she loosened up a bit, she might be cute.

"Mark? You need any help?" Lisa, the librarian, asked as Mark stood up.

Lisa was the last person he'd ever imagine as a librarian. She had a cheerful smile, rarely shushed people, and wore her long blond hair down in flowing waves. Her attractiveness had doubled library use among single males in Carterville. Thankfully, she was closer to his mother's age than his, so Minnie hadn't tried to set him up with her yet.

"No. I'm just looking around."

Lisa glanced at the shelves. "Business books aren't usually your style. I thought you preferred woodworking and John Sandford."

"I need something on bookkeeping. I need to get all my stuff together, especially with taxes being due soon." Mark shook his head at the shelves.

"You're in the right spot." She tapped the spines of the books. "What you need should be here. We also have a booklet and a CD-ROM from the state that might help. I'll grab them for you."

"The booklet would be great, but you can keep the CD-ROM. I don't have a computer yet." He followed Lisa to a wall of brochures. She ran a finger across the Plexiglass display boxes until she found the one she wanted.

"You don't have a computer yet?" Lisa asked, handing him a glossy booklet.

"I hoped to buy one during the sales after Christmas, but

a couple jobs I had fell through. People blew their wad at Christmas and decided to delay their remodeling projects for a month or two. It leaves me without any extra cash."

"Didn't Minnie offer to buy you one?" Lisa asked.

"Yeah. I wouldn't let her. She does too much for me already."

Lisa pulled a book off the shelf and handed it to him. "This should help. I'll get one of the CD-ROMs for you, too. You'll get a computer soon, and then you'll need it."

Mark flipped through the book. "May I use one of the computers? I promised Minnie I'd check on eBay for some of the furnishings she wanted."

"Minnie likes eBay, doesn't she?" Lisa smiled.

"Yeah, she doesn't understand how it works, but she thinks you can get anything there."

As Mark pulled out a chair and settled himself at a computer, Lisa added, "You know, I could help you set up a profile at Matchmaker. I can practically do them in my sleep."

Mark kept himself from rolling his eyes. "No thanks."

"When you are interested, let me know. I've discovered all the secrets for creating a good profile." Lisa wandered away to do whatever she did all day besides setting people up.

Mark stared at the screen. Why did the Library Ladies think he needed to date someone? He especially didn't want to meet anyone online. Everyone lied in their profile, so what good would it do? They wouldn't be the same person in person. And who really liked long walks on the beach?

When he was ready to date, he'd rather meet someone

in person. See if there was a spark. Get to know the real person. People could make themselves out to be anything online.

He didn't have the time or money for a girlfriend right now anyway. Once he got his construction business going, maybe. He needed to get his name out there and get a few more big jobs. That would help him more than shelling out a couple hundred dollars for advertising in the newspaper. Unless it was a coupon for a half-price Family Special at Bart's Sandwich Shop, he doubted anyone even looked at the advertisements.

He had a couple of small jobs lined up. Maybe those would lead to more. Until then, he had Minnie's place to keep him working.

He pulled a sticky note out of his wallet and stuck it on the computer screen. Minnie had given him the list of light fixtures she wanted. He'd barely finished punching the first one into the eBay search field, when he was slapped on the back. He coughed and turned to see who his attacker was.

"Thanks, Bryce. I thought I was going to choke on all the air I was breathing."

Bryce tugged the chair away from the adjoining computer and sat down. Grease permanently stained his overalls and lined his fingernails. He hid his crew cut under a Valvoline hat. "How's it going?"

"Just checking on some stuff for Minnie. She thinks eBay is the only place to shop now. She won't let me buy anything from a store until I price-check it here first." Mark scrolled through the search results and clicked on a promising listing.

"What's she got you looking for now? More black toilets?"

"Light fixtures. I found some cheap ones at a resale shop, but she doesn't like them. Says they're offensive. Look too much like female anatomy." Mark rolled his eyes. "What are you doing here?"

"Judi had a meeting at school, so I had to bring Boppy to story time." He pushed his cap back and scratched his forehead.

"When are you going to stop calling him that? It's dumb. He'll be mental before he's four years old."

"We can't have two Bryces in the house. Judi yells my name enough. This way I know when to ignore her."

"I'm sure she appreciates that," Mark said, clicking on another auction listing.

Bryce shrugged. "I listen when it's important. Like when she says, 'Bryce, I'm going to bed.' I'm all over that."

Mark glanced at the computer screen and clicked on one of the auctions. "How's your car coming?"

"I adjusted the valves, but it still knocks. I've got three weeks before the race to get it straightened out. I'm also playing with the size of my tires. I think I can corner better with smaller ones on the inside. All this snow stinks, though. I can't do any good test runs until the arena is ready. No place outside to try it out."

"You don't think you've got it in the bag this year?"

"Competition's always tough. Never let your guard down. Hey, while I'm thinking of it . . ." He leaned forward and pulled his wallet out of his back pocket. He flipped it open, withdrew two tickets, and handed them to Mark. "I got a couple extra tickets with my entrance fee. The rest of the guys are getting in with the pit crew, so I thought you could use them."

"Thanks." Mark reached for the tickets. They were curled from the fold in Bryce's wallet. "I only need one."

"Take 'em both. You never know." Bryce winked at him.

Mark pressed his lips tightly together and counted. When he was calm, he asked, "What craft do you bring to the Ladies' Night Out gatherings? You could always make jewelry out of petrified bird crap like that guy I saw on the *Tonight Show* a couple years ago."

"Very funny. The race is three weeks away," Bryce insisted, pushing the extra ticket back at Mark. "Lots of things can happen between now and then."

Mark took the tickets and stuffed them into his wallet. "The most beautiful woman I've ever seen is not going to end up in Carterville solely to go on a date with me. Let me know if you need the extra one back. I'm sure it won't get used, and it's a shame to waste it."

"Hey, if you don't find someone to use it, scalp it at the gate. Do what you like." Bryce rolled his eyes and leaned forward to peek at the clock on Mark's computer. "Boppy'll be in there for another twenty minutes. What do the other parents do around here while they wait?" He tilted his chair back on two legs and drummed his fingers on the table.

"Some people can read, and they like books. I'm surprised they let you leave Boppy in story time by himself.

That kid's on a permanent sugar rush. They do have some books with pictures of cars in them. Lisa could show you where they are."

Bryce snorted. "I'll pass. I'd need Boppy to read them to me anyway," he said sarcastically.

Mark found several of the things on Minnie's list. The auctions had a couple of days to go, so he added them to his watch list.

"I heard you have a new boss at the tax place," Bryce said, tracing the broken edge of one fingernail along the wood grain on the table. "Is she pretty?"

This was it. This was why Bryce was badgering him, why he thought Mark might need an extra ticket to the race.

Mark made some notes on his list before answering. "Yeah, some uptight career woman from the big city. She spends all day tapping away on her laptop."

"A woman, huh? Is she hot?" That would be the only thing that concerned Bryce.

Mark sighed. As if Bryce hadn't known the new manager was a woman. Leslie had been in town nearly twenty-four hours. Enough time in Carterville for Bryce to learn her measurements. "She has brown hair she wears all twisted up, and I've seen more warmth in a tray of ice cubes. I'm not asking her out."

"I wasn't suggesting it." Bryce shook his head; then he rocked his chair forward and leaned toward Mark. "But you could use a date to the race."

Mark considered elbowing Bryce in the nose. "She wouldn't be interested. In me or the race. I don't think her shoes have even touched dirt."

"How long do you think she'll last here?"

Mark shook his head. "I think she wants to get back to headquarters as soon as possible. She won't be in town one minute longer than she's required to be."

"If the Library Ladies know that, maybe they'll leave her alone," Bryce said.

"I'd be happy if they left me alone," Mark mumbled, closing the window on the screen and tossing the golf pencil back into its basket.

"There's only one way to make that happen," Bryce reminded him.

"I'm not dating anyone just for their sake." Mark stood and pushed his chair in.

"At least you don't have to worry about them setting you up with your boss. If she's leaving town, they won't be interested."

Mark wasn't sure anything short of death would dissuade the Ladies, but it did give him hope.

Chapter Two

Leslie flipped the dead bolt on the inside of her door with a sigh of relief. She didn't think the lace-edged DO NOT DISTURB door hanger would actually keep Minnie out. From what she gathered, this was the off-season for tourists—tourists?—and Minnie missed having guests at the Lilac Bower. Minnie had chattered continuously from the moment Leslie stepped through the door and fussed over her like a long-lost granddaughter. In all the chatter, Leslie hadn't heard what caused the tourists to flock to this small town, but she had passed some kind of sports complex on the way into town, so maybe there was a tractor pull or something. She shuddered to think what the *or something* might be. She doubted anyone interested in a tractor pull would find the Lilac Bower to his or her taste. Actually she didn't know anyone under seventy who would find the room she was in to their taste.

18

Leslie wheeled her suitcase next to the dresser and placed her laptop case and purse on a chair. Crocheted doilies in white, beige, or lilac graced every surface. Lace fringed the curtains, the bedspread, and every one of the sixteen purple pillows piled on the bed. Decoupaged cards hung on the walls, and on top of the dresser was a pair of age-colored gloves with a string of pearls draped artfully around a tea cup, saucer, and plate featuring a lilac pattern. It was like stepping into a Victorian tea-room.

She pushed the bathroom door open, bracing herself for a fluffy purple toilet cover cozy fringed with lace and one of those crocheted dolls her grandmother put over the spare roll of toilet paper.

She froze with the door partway open. The door swung back toward her, but she put a hand out to stop its forward motion and stepped into the room. After looking around in amazement, she leaned back into her room and looked around for another door.

Surely this bathroom was not the intended one for this room. But she saw no other possibility, even after studying the wallpaper for a camouflaged door.

Turning back to the bathroom, she gaped at a Kohler salesperson's dream. Water trickled out of a spout on the wall into a large basin that sat halfway out of the counter. There was a Jacuzzi tub with a similar faucet as well as a separate shower with—she counted audibly, pulling open the glass door—six heads. All of the fixtures including the toilet were slate in color. A luxurious chaise lounge with an inviting chenille blanket draped across it sat in a corner surrounded by candles.

Beside the Jacuzzi was a little basket of bath products. Bubble bath, shampoo, shower gel, a glass container of bath salts, and . . . a little black book? Leslie eased the book from between the bottles and flipped to the title page. She almost dropped it after reading the title. *The Encyclopedia of Romance: 101 Ways to Heat up Your Love Life*. Leslie slammed the cover shut. One of the previous guests must have left it here. Leslie couldn't imagine the energetic but definitely grandmotherly Minnie purchasing it.

Leslie tucked the book back into the basket under the bath salts and shampoo. She didn't want to cause Minnie a heart attack. She started to toss it toward the wastebasket but stopped. She couldn't throw it away. Minnie would think it was hers and throw her out of the bed-and-breakfast. Leslie hid the little book in her purse. She'd toss it into the garbage at the office.

Leslie kicked off her shoes, removed the mountain of lace-covered pillows from the bed, and flopped down onto it. She thumbed the remote and found a Hallmark movie. Her only option to extricate herself from this mess was to turn the Carterville branch around. She intended to court corporate clients and convert this office from a seasonal tax service to a year-round accounting office. Corporate clients would provide business throughout the year and improve the branch's standing at headquarters. If she successfully turned the office around, she'd restore her reputation as well.

Leslie spent the next morning slogging through the client files and correspondence overflowing her in-box.

She managed to stop the fax machine from chirping every few minutes by reminding headquarters she actually used e-mail. She also learned that Mr. Perkins hadn't filed any tax returns electronically last year. He'd informed customers there'd be an extra charge for the service, and many customers went elsewhere. Even though Mr. Perkins ignored some of the newer services, Mr. Hanston had promised him a job until he retired, and Mr. Hanston always kept his word.

From the look of his desk, Perkins should have retired years ago. Leslie found no rhyme or reason to piles of papers on the desk. Three-year-old tax returns and faded faxes on thermal paper were intermingled with newspapers and reports from last fall. She tossed much of the paper straight into the bin for shredding.

Leslie tried to file some of the folders, but the file cabinet drawers were either jammed full, jammed shut, or so disorganized that placing files in them would be as useful as shredding them.

She was reaching for the stack of papers in the outbox when the phone rang. The ring was one of those old-fashioned bell styles, and she wasn't sure what it was at first. Shoving aside stacks of papers, she tried to remember if she'd actually seen a phone on the desk. By the fourth ring, she managed to find the coiled cord and follow it to the receiver.

"Hanston and Boyd Accounting. How may I help you?" she said breathlessly.

"Leslie?" the voice on the other end asked.

"Yes. This is she." She opened the call record file on her laptop and poised her fingers to type notes.

"Hi. This is Minnie."

Her fingers left the keyboard. Leslie sighed and adjusted the receiver between her ear and her shoulder.

"Is something wrong?" Leslie remembered the book in her purse and made another mental note to toss it into the garbage.

"No. No. Not at all. This isn't about business. I missed you this morning, and I wanted to know if you had plans for tonight."

"I have a lot of paperwork to sort out. I was going to pop out for something to eat and then get back to it. You don't have to hold dinner for me. I know you said you would, but it isn't necessary."

"You've been working long hours all week. I thought you might need a break. A bunch of my friends are getting together tonight."

Leslie could sense Minnie's disappointment. "Thanks, but I've got a lot to do." But there's no hurry, her conscience nagged her. The paperwork organization could wait. The files obviously wouldn't combust if they weren't filed by a certain time.

"Well, if you change your mind, we're meeting at the library for our weekly Ladies' Night Out. Everyone usually brings a craft project to work on."

Crafts? The only crafts Leslie remembered doing involved gluing macaroni and peas to construction paper.

"I don't do crafts." Leslie glanced at the clock. "Thanks anyway."

"You're welcome to come if you change your mind."

Leslie hung up the phone and leaned back in her chair.

Her behind had been planted in her desk chair for over four hours. She stood up, pressing her palms into the small of her back, stretching her neck, and rolling her shoulders. Usually she didn't sit still for quite so long; she was either meeting with clients or chatting with co-workers while walking back and forth to the coffee machine and the bathroom.

An evening of relaxation sounded good. Maybe in her Jacuzzi tub. Or she should take up Minnie's offer and go to the library program and get to know some of the people in Carterville. It wasn't as if it would make her any more of a dork, spending Friday night at the library with a bunch of older women watching them crochet—was that even the right term?—toilet paper cozies. She might as well watch the dust collect on these files. It'd be just as exciting.

Leslie finally decided to order in pizza and work through the rest of the evening. She had so much to do to prepare the office for the upcoming tax season. She'd spent all her time so far trying to unearth the surface of her desk. She still needed to develop a marketing plan to attract business clients as well. That was the only way to turn this branch around.

She reached for the phone to place her pizza order, but it jangled just as she touched the receiver.

"Hello, Hanston and Boyd Accounting."

"They've got you answering the phone there? Aren't you supposed to be in charge?"

Chuck. Leslie wished the old telephone commercials about reaching out and touching someone were literal, because she would like to reach out and smack Chuck Silverman alongside the head with the clunky handset of this phone.

"My receptionist has the day off," she replied with affected lightness.

"You're all by yourself? Must be some place." Chuck barked a laugh.

"Something like that." Chuck knew she was ticked off by her transfer. She'd been next in line for the promotion he somehow got. Something strange was brewing at headquarters.

"Trying to stimulate loyalty to the new boss by giving your receptionist the day off?"

She imagined Chuck checking out his blond spiked hair in the reflection of his nameplate. "What did you need, Chuck? I have a lot of paperwork to finish."

"I wanted to see how your new position was treating you."

She thought she could hear him sniggering. "It's fine. I'm quite busy, you know," she said between clenched teeth.

"Doing what? Polishing your nails? Really, Leslie, we both know how much work is involved in running that branch."

"Yes." She decided to ignore his patronizing tone. "I'm absolutely inundated with paperwork." He didn't need to know that most of it only needed to be filed. "I suppose I should thank you for the 'promotion.' Without your influence, I never would have made branch manager." She paused, trying to sound naive and innocent, but she knew sarcasm edged her voice. "Especially in Carteraville. You must have used all the cards in your deck to get this for me."

"Am I sensing bitterness, Leslie?"

His bitterness radar should have melted under the heat by now.

"Whatever would I have to be bitter about, Chuck? I've gotten a promotion. I am a branch manager now. Never mind that this branch is the smallest and least prestigious, not to mention least profitable, in the whole company and that I had more clients and billing dollars in my previous position than I do now."

"What did I have to do with that?"

Leslie wanted to reach through the phone and grab that little metrosexual diamond stud earring and rip it from his earlobe.

"What indeed? You knew I was a shoo-in for your new job, and you wanted me out of the way. I know you talked with Ms. Boyd about me." He did more than talk with Ms. Boyd, but Leslie doubted she had been the topic of many of their interactions.

"You always were jealous, Leslie."

Leslie imagined him doing that stupid thing with his tie, flipping it onto his nose and blowing it off. He always did that when he was tired of a conversation on the phone. "Standoffish, too. That's why you never had a date for the office parties."

"My personal life is none of your business." She spat out the last word. Actually, it wasn't anyone's business, because it didn't exist.

"I hope you don't get too bored in Carterville. Watched any Hallmark movies lately?"

"For your information, I have plans tonight. I must go and get ready." She hung up the phone, hoping the click echoed in Chuck's ear. She wasn't going to take the chance he'd call back tonight or track her down at the bed-and-breakfast. She picked up the phone and punched in Minnie's number.

When Minnie's scratchy voice answered, Leslie quickly interrupted. "Minnie, I'll be there in a few minutes, but I need a craft."

Chapter Three

"**I**'m so glad you decided to come," said Minnie as she whipped her Buick Century into a parking spot behind the library.

Minnie had hurried Leslie directly to her car when she arrived at the Lilac Bower, not even letting her run upstairs to change her clothes.

"You needed to get out. You've been working so hard this week. And it's so hard to meet people here. There aren't a lot of good places for young folks like yourself to go. Besides, you're saving me. I've gotten tired of Edith's rambling on about her new daughter-in-law, Wendy, and how fantastic she is. So you will give us a new topic of conversation."

"New topic?" Leslie squeaked. She'd hoped to hide in a corner with the bag that looked like her mother's couch cushion and pretend to do something with whatever was inside. She definitely did not want to be the topic of conversation.

"Wendy is a nice girl and all, but you can only rehash a success so many times."

"I don't want to be the center of attention. I came to relax. People aren't going to gang up on me and ask all kinds of questions, are they?"

Minnie laughed, ducking back into the car to retrieve a plastic tub. "Edith credits the group for introducing the couple." She hefted the tub and slammed the door shut with her hip. "Someone just needed to get her son off his behind and get him looking."

"This Wendy did that?" Leslie was certain she'd missed something in this conversation.

"With the proper assistance."

Leslie scurried to open the door of the library and then followed Minnie down a hallway. The head of a worm painted on the wall greeted them at the door. Its body stretched down the hallway in segments of paper "books."

"I suppose Wendy's nice enough, but she sure didn't look it when she arrived in town. Oh, good, Lisa brought her fruit salad." Minnie led Leslie into a medium-sized meeting room. The room was arranged with over-stuffed chairs surrounding a glowing gas fireplace at one end. Several women had scraps of paper and fabric and twisted piles of thread spread out on TV trays in front of their chairs. Leslie clutched her bag tightly. She hoped Minnie had given her something she could reasonably pretend to do. Especially since she doubted Minnie packed any Elmer's glue or macaroni.

Minnie abandoned her for the food table. If this had been a tax conference, Leslie would have worked the room, questioning each of the women about their offices, the number of returns they averaged, etc. But here she wasn't sure what to do. She didn't want to latch on to Minnie all night, but she didn't want to sit by herself in a corner either, even though that's what she'd professed only a few moments earlier. She ventured over to the food table, where Minnie was filling a snack plate with the fruit salad and chatting with a woman who ladled pink punch into plastic cups and another woman who arranged cookies on a tray.

Minnie shoved a plate toward Leslie. "Try the fruit salad. Edith, Lisa, this is Leslie. She's staying in the Lilac Room."

Leslie smiled and shook hands with the matchmaking Edith. Edith was a tall, chubby woman with bouncy red-dyed curls. She was wearing a sweater with snowmen across the front.

Lisa had long, wavy blond hair and was sampling one of the sugar-sprinkled confections.

"The Lilac Room, huh?" Edith grimaced as if she'd bit into a sour grape. "I'm sorry. Minnie needs to get that room redecorated. I don't know why she didn't start the renovations there. It's atrocious."

Leslie glanced at Minnie, expecting her to look miffed at the other woman's comments. Minnie stuffed her mouth with another spoonful of fruit salad.

"The room is quite comfortable and well-coordinated," Leslie said, trying to be diplomatic.

"I take it you haven't seen her redesign sketches. It'll

be fabulous when it's finished." Edith pressed a hand to her chest. "I've thought about staying there myself."

"You can't until Mark finishes the rest of the rooms. And he's waiting for the electrician to finish wiring the new light fixtures," Minnie said through a mouthful of salad.

"I think the designs are just amazing. So sleek and modern. Very daring. I love it." Lisa clapped her hands together.

"My bathroom must be part of the redesign." Leslie scooped some fruit salad. Licking her spoon, she understood Minnie's raptures. The salad was the perfect blend of sweetness and marshmallowy goodness.

Minnie nodded. "Mark got a deal on all the fixtures, so I had to do the bathrooms first. He uses the computer and the eBay or something."

"What made you decide to remodel?" Leslie asked, accepting a glass of punch from Edith.

"I couldn't stand the existing decorating, and there were some problems with the plaster and fixtures. The roof leaked, damaging the ceilings in two of the rooms and dissolving the wallpaper. I couldn't wait to get to work."

"You're new to the bed-and-breakfast industry, then?"

"It's been an adventure. It's only been a year; but business has been steady, despite the remodeling dust and Mark's traipsing in and out all the time."

Leslie guessed many guests would put up with a lot more than drywall dust for a chance to see Mark at work. She hadn't seen him at the bed-and-breakfast, but she'd locked herself in her room to hide from Minnie each night.

Minnie described how she'd decided to purchase the bed-and-breakfast and some of the challenges she'd faced with taxes and licenses.

Talking business—Leslie sighed—*comfortable ground.* She filled her plate with cookies and, of course, more fruit salad. Chatting about business issues, she followed Minnie to a circle of chairs. She dropped her bag onto the floor next to her chair and tugged a TV tray into place. Nodding at something Minnie was saying about government regulations, she took a sip of the punch.

Her eyes flew open, and she coughed, sending punch up her nose.

"The punch is spiked," she gasped when the burning subsided.

"Shh!" Minnie hissed. "Someone might overhear. Nobody's supposed to say anything. The library doesn't allow alcohol in the building."

"Why not meet somewhere else?" Leslie asked after blowing her nose into her napkin.

"We used to meet at the Lilac Bower, but with the renovations, there isn't enough room to spread out." Minnie raised her cup. "And we couldn't go without any. This is our night out."

"Ladies! May I have your attention please?" Edith's voice rang above the murmur of the other conversations. "We have a new guest. Leslie, would you stand up?"

Leslie grabbed her punch, took a long drink, then half stood and waved.

"Welcome to our group!" Several of the women nodded and smiled. Six women sat around the fireplace, each ensconced in the paraphernalia of her chosen craft.

Leslie opened her bag and reached in. She pulled out fuzzy yarn and sticks. Knitting? One of her co-workers in the city had jumped on the craze when some celebrity started. The friend made a small scarf that unraveled as soon as she took it off the needles. Her friend had tried to teach Leslie, insisting she would find it soothing. Ha. She'd ended up with a ball of yarn so tangled, she swore there were no ends to work with.

Leslie picked up the ball. It was blue and green variegated angora. Her favorite colors. If she couldn't knit, at least she could touch the yarn. It was one of the softest textures she'd ever felt.

Minnie had also packed a book on knitting and a laminated diagram of stitches. Leslie flipped through the projects in the book until she found one with only one star next to the difficulty level. It was a long scarf without any ruffles or holes. Still fingering the yarn, she studied the instructions. What was with all the letters? Couldn't they spell things out? K1, P2? What did that mean?

Edith was jabbering on about club business. Leslie heard her mention projects and a charity. Leslie turned back to the beginning of the book and found several diagrams of the knitting process. She studied them closely but wasn't sure they would ever be replicated on her set of needles.

"So, have fun with your projects, and don't forget to say hi to Leslie," Edith finally finished.

Leslie's head popped up at the mention of her name.

"Where are you from?" the woman on her right asked. She studied Leslie over the tops of her tiny drugstore glasses. A carousel of scissors with multicolored handles and a stack of paper surrounded her. Leslie was taken aback by the directness of the question.

"I was transferred here temporarily from the corporate office of Hanston and Boyd Accounting in Chicago." It was only a partial lie, Leslie told herself. They didn't need to know that Hanston and Boyd—or, more likely, Chuck—intended this as a permanent change. "What are you working on?" Leslie asked.

"My name's Dinah. I'm scrapbooking a baby book for my grandson. His mother is too busy, so I'm trying it out. I am not very creative, but I love these scissors. Each one cuts with a different edge. This one does scallops. This one does a zigzag, and this one is my favorite—it does an edge that looks like a tear." Dinah clicked the scissors open and closed a couple of times. "Have you ever done scrapbooking?"

Before Leslie could answer, Dinah shoved a stack of pictures into her hand. "This is my grandson, Boppy. He's eighteen months old."

"Boppy?" Leslie flipped through the pictures as quickly as politeness would allow.

"Isn't that an awful nickname?" Dinah clipped the edge of a blue polka-dotted paper. "It's short for Bryson Paul. Isn't he a sweetie?"

The camera had caught a little gleam in his eye that made Leslie believe he could wrap any mildly suscepti-ble adult around his little finger, especially his grand-mother. "I'm sure he is."

"He is the spitting image of my son."

Leslie hoped she didn't mean that her son walked

around in droopy diapers with green beans smeared across his chest, which was what Boppy—poor kid— seemed to be doing in every single picture.

"You will have to meet my daughter-in-law. She's about your age. Bryce and Judi got together shortly after we started meeting. Almost five years ago already."

"Has it really been that long?" the woman next to her responded. She rested her needle and scraps of fabric in her lap.

"We might have to make this a business. One hundred percent success rate," chimed Edith. "Well, one hundred percent as long as we don't count Paula."

"But she couldn't be helped," said Edith.

Several of the women nodded in agreement.

They would say the same about me if they saw me attempt to knit, Leslie thought. She set the pictures down on the tray. It was more enjoyable to see what other people were making than tangling her fingers in yarn anyway.

"I'm Yvonne," a woman said with a needle clenched between her teeth and gigantic glasses perched on the end of her nose. A beaded lanyard trailed from the bows on her glasses and around her helmet of iron gray curls. Yvonne had several squares of green fabric with animal shapes pinned to them.

"What are you making?" Leslie asked, taking a sip of her punch.

"This is for my future niece. She's due in a month."

"Congratulations. Your family must be very excited."

"Indeed it is." Yvonne set her project in her lap. "We'd given up hope of Trixie's ever getting married, but last summer it all worked out, and now we have a baby on the way. My sister, Betty, is beside herself with excitement. This will be her first grandchild, and she has purchased every baby toy there is."

"No, I haven't," called a woman in a burgundy velour sweat suit from the entryway. "Sorry I'm late. Cal needed supper. I haven't bought the battery-powered Hummer parked outside Little Tots."

"But she already has the Barbie Jeep. They're pretty sure the baby is a girl," Edith added.

"Why didn't you make Cal fend for himself?" asked Minnie, bringing Betty a glass of punch. "He can heat up a pizza."

"Yeah, I know," answered Betty. "But then I would have to clean the oven afterward. The man may be able to teach physics, but setting an oven timer is impossible. I don't know how he survived as a bachelor for so long."

"Betty and Cal were married in a double wedding with her daughter, Trixie," Minnie informed Leslie. "It was the event of the summer. Was there any resident of Carterville who wasn't there?"

"Probably not. I even invited Yvonne, and she's the only one I would have left off the list." Betty plunked her canvas bag onto the TV tray beside Yvonne's quilt squares. She patted Yvonne on the shoulder and sat in the chair next to her. She extracted scissors, pincushion, thimble, and a mass of folded fabric.

"I shouldn't have come, with the atrocious bridesmaid dress you made me wear. The things you'll do for a sister." Yvonne bit off a thread and pushed her needle into the fabric. "I thought your taste had gotten better over the last twenty-five years."

"I thought the dresses were quite pretty," said Minnie.

"You didn't have to wear one," grumbled Yvonne, scowling at Minnie. "Itchy and hot."

"What did they look like?" asked Leslie, intrigued by this group and willing to ask whatever questions necessary to keep their focus away from herself. She was starting to suspect that Minnie had an ulterior motive in inviting her.

"My daughter wanted a theme wedding, and, even though we are midwesterners through and through, she wanted a Deep South *Gone With the Wind* theme. We all had hoop skirts, corsets, and parasols—the whole she-bang. And, boy, were they ever hot."

"The temperature was a record high for the month of June," reminded Betty.

"We had full-length gloves, too. Black ones," said Yvonne.

"What color were the dresses?" Leslie asked, pushing her TV tray away, her knitting completely forgotten.

"Yvonne thinks Trixie shouldn't have worn white, but I say, it's her wedding day, she can do what she wants. She had white gloves, too." Betty favored Yvonne with a pointed look. "My dress was light blue, and the other bridesmaids' dresses were mulberry."

"In case you were wondering, mulberry absorbs heat from the sun like nothing else, and hoops act as insulators. Throw in the fact you're already suffocating in a corset . . ." Yvonne shook her head. "I swore the fat was melting off my thighs and puddling in my shoes."

"What fat?" asked Edith, shifting in her chair. She

was knitting faster than Leslie had ever seen needles move—not that she'd seen many people knit besides her co-worker and the instructor on the video. Whatever was on Edith's needles grew by inches.

"Well, it's gone now," Yvonne said, shaking a pair of scissors in Edith's direction. "Melted right off, and I never gained it back."

Leslie couldn't help herself; she burst out laughing. She suddenly had a mental picture of a very large Yvonne melting into a puddle.

"I lost at least ten pounds," Yvonne insisted.

"Yvonne's always been as thin as a rail," said Dinah, shaking her head.

"What about you, Betty?" Leslie asked. "Did you lose weight, too?"

"I don't recall. If I did, it quickly found its way back home." She laughed, snapping the elastic waistband of her jogging pants.

"I must admit, the dresses wouldn't have been so bad if it hadn't been a hundred and ten degrees in the shade with one hundred percent humidity. We'd have looked every bit like Scarlett O'Hara and not like magnolias three days past their full bloom."

"You'll have to show me pictures sometime."

"I think I have some in my box." Dinah started digging through the Tupperware container of photos she'd brought. She extracted a stack of pictures with a pink ribbon tied around them.

"These are all our weddings." Dinah brought them over to Leslie, pulling the ribbon loose from the packet. "I'm going to do a book sometime."

"When she finishes the pictures of Boppy," said Lisa. "The rest of that container is full of them."

"I'll get to it," Dinah said. Then she glanced at the box and sighed. "Someday."

Leslie started flipping through the pictures.

"That's Dinah's son, Bryson, and his wife, Judi."

Leslie made appropriate comments about each of the bride's dresses and the flowers or the handsomeness of the groom. The ladies around her named each of the subjects and when the wedding was.

"All these weddings in the last five years," Leslie commented. "This town must be a singles' Mecca."

"It didn't used to be," said Edith.

"We despaired of any of those young people ever settling down and getting married," said Betty.

"Except Betty," said Yvonne.

"Yeah, that one was a surprise to us, too," said Edith.

"I knew it would happen," Dinah said.

"No, you made a lucky guess. Cal was a confirmed bachelor," said Lisa.

"A man is not a confirmed bachelor until he is dead," Minnie said.

"Well, we didn't despair of Betty's *ever* getting married because she'd already been married once," said Edith.

"But we weren't expecting her to get married again," said Minnie.

"She didn't need our help to sweep Cal off his feet," Dinah said.

"I would think he was so tired of peanut butter and

jelly sandwiches that anyone with a warm meal'd be able to sweep him off his feet," said Yvonne.

"Cal is a fine man," said Betty.

"I didn't say he wasn't. He can't cook," replied Yvonne.

"Hold up a second," Leslie said, raising a hand. "What do you mean by needing 'your help'?"

The Library Ladies suddenly went quiet. All the craft projects were forgotten. The clink of needles dropping onto TV trays echoed through the room. They kept looking at one another, trying to find the one best able to explain. Several moments passed, and the room was the quietest it had been since Leslie and Minnie arrived.

Finally, Edith cleared her throat. "What you are about to hear does not leave this room."

Chapter Four

Yvonne jumped from her seat and hurried to the meeting-room door. She kicked the wooden stop and swung the door shut.

"A few years ago, we realized there were several young people of our relation who seemed to be missing out on golden opportunities right here in town. Lisa—she's the librarian—saw all these young people coming into the library with similar interests, but they never met."

"They were into online dating," Lisa said. "One guy even set up a profile on a mail-order Russian bride site."

"Years ago, the Ladies' Night Out group met as a social club to enjoy crafts and gossip. Anyway . . . Lisa told us about all these lost singles."

"They weren't opening their eyes to what was around them. We decided to help by connecting them," said Edith.

"Bryce and Judi were first, and we've had many successes since," said Dinah.

"But they don't know we're . . . what's the word?" Edith snapped her fingers.

"Interfering?" Leslie offered.

"Intervening," supplied Lisa.

"It's all completely natural," said Minnie, waving a hand.

"None of these people know what you're doing?" Leslie flapped the stack of pictures. These women were delusional. How could anyone not know?

"Nope. We're very subtle," Yvonne said.

"We have a one hundred percent success rate," said Yvonne.

"Ninety-nine percent," reminded Minnie. "There's still one project we haven't figured out. He may be the death of our mission."

"We shouldn't count Paula. You can't work with someone like that. We'd be obligated to stop if he actually married her."

"What happened?" Leslie asked.

"There was this new girl in town. She seemed very nice, very energetic, always working on some new project. And we thought about arranging something with Mark. He's got four jobs or something. They both liked to be on the go."

"I think they went out once, and then Paula was arrested."

"I heard she ran naked down Main Street," said Lisa.

"No, she bit the sheriff when he handcuffed her."

"He still has a scar. It's on his shoulder." Betty traced

a half circle on her left shoulder. "She gnawed right through his uniform."

"She's still in the mental hospital."

"I hope she never gets out." Yvonne shook her head.

Minnie sighed and folded her napkin. "Mark hasn't dated anyone since."

"We've tried subtle suggestions," said Edith, shaking her knitting.

"He's such a nice young man. Always willing to help." Yvonne snipped a thread. "I like calling him to move things for me. Such a sweetie."

"I wish we could find someone for him," said Minnie. "But there hasn't been anyone new in town lately."

A nervous tingle traveled up Leslie's spine.

"And he's usually too busy to get out and meet new people."

The uncomfortable tingle grew to a decided itch. She could see where this was going. She took a gulp of her punch.

"We should try harder," said Betty.

"I would like to see him settled and married," Minnie said. "He's the only family I've got."

Wondering how she might divert conversation, Leslie drained her glass.

"Leslie dear, are you dating anyone?"

Leslie choked. Her eyes streamed tears. Punch dribbled out her nose.

"Leslie, are you okay?" Minnie asked, handing her a napkin.

Leslie wiped her face and hands, searching frantically for an answer that wouldn't make her their next prey.

She didn't want small-town life. She wanted to climb the corporate ladder and shove her fist through the glass ceiling. She didn't have time to date.

She wanted multimillion dollar accounts and influential clients. None of that was possible in Carterville. She planned do her job, put in her time, and finally get the promotion she deserved.

The women were staring at her expectantly.

"Not really," she said reluctantly. "But," she added, when the women scooted to the edges of their seats, "the only men I've met have been work associates, and I prefer to keep my professional and personal lives separate."

They weren't sliding back! Yvonne and Betty tilted their heads.

"I'd like to focus on my career right now," Leslie said, scrambling for something to divert them.

"You know, I watched that Hitch movie, and he said that when women say that, it's a load of crap," said Betty.

Leslie's jaw dropped open. She never expected a word like *crap* to drop from Betty's grandmotherly lips.

"That's so true," Yvonne said. "Every woman has time for both."

"I don't," Leslie protested. "I'm swamped with paperwork, and tax season is coming up. . . ."

"Taxes? It's that time already?" Edith grumbled. "I'd better stock up on antacids."

Thankfully for Leslie the conversation drifted to the advantages of various home remedies for heartburn and away from the nonexistence of her love life.

Chapter Five

Leslie jammed her key into the lock and attempted to twist it. It didn't move. She pulled it out and checked the symbol. It matched the lock, so she tried again. The key turned a little and stuck again. Leslie glanced around, hoping no one saw her fumbling.

Typical Monday, blinding sun and freezing cold on the same day. This only happened in Michigan. She yanked off her leather gloves and stuffed them into her coat pocket. She pushed her sunglasses on top of her head. She could feel the heat rising on her neck. How dumb was she? She couldn't open a simple lock.

She grasped the cold doorknob and jammed the key back into the lock and tried to twist it again.

Nothing.

Dropping her shoulder bag and purse to the salted sidewalk, she took a deep breath, watching it hang in the frosty air. She could prepare a financial analysis of a multimillion dollar company; she could open a locked door.

She applied the key to the lock again.

"Good morning," a deep voice said over her shoulder.

She turned, shielding her eyes with one hand. "Hey, Mark. I didn't realize you'd be back today."

"The ceiling tiles finally came in, so I can restore the ceiling to its former glory." He smiled. "If we add thirty years of smoke and dirt to them, they'll match the others."

Mark wore a gray sweatshirt with a faded Special Olympics logo. His worn jeans were paint-splattered and dragging white strings around his work boots. Leslie knew women who paid over $500 for jeans like his. She shook her head slightly. She'd spent her entire weekend trying to avoid thinking about Mark. The ladies at the library were responsible for that. When she wasn't avoiding Minnie and her well-intentioned but prying questions, she was trying to shove the image of his friendly grin out of her mind.

"We can't have everything." She shrugged.

Mark shoved his hands into his pockets. "How are things going? Are you settling in?"

With his eyes focused directly on her, her cheeks burned from more than the January wind.

"Okay." She reached up to smooth her hair, smacking herself in the face with her keys. "There's a lot of paperwork to sort."

She fidgeted with an earring. Then, feeling self-conscious, she dropped her hand and crossed her arms across her chest. Wasn't touching your face and hair the first rule in the flirting manual to show your interest?

What was she doing? She mentally cursed Minnie for the direction of her thoughts. She wasn't interested in dating anyone, Mark included.

"Shall we go in? I'd like to get to work." He gestured toward the door.

"Yeah." Leslie half smiled and shoved the key into the lock, praying this time the lock would pop open. The key remained stubbornly in place.

Warped door? Sure. The lock was solid metal. She stomped her foot. What kind of moron would he think she was? Not that it mattered what he thought of her.

"Need a hand?" he asked, leaning over her shoulder. The fresh scent of cedar wafted over her.

"The lock's frozen or something." She dropped her keys into his outstretched palm. "Maybe you can get it."

He stepped around her. "Moisture drips down the door from the hole in the canopy all the time. It gets into the lock and freezes overnight. It's a pain."

"Repair the canopy," she mumbled. "Another thing to put on my list."

"Got it." He pushed the door open with one arm and motioned for her to enter. She grabbed her purse and briefcase and scurried past him.

"What'd you do? I would have been standing there all day."

"Sometimes it helps to keep turning the key back and forth. It creates friction and melts the ice." He shrugged. "Either that or hope you get lucky."

Lucky? She coughed. "Thanks."

Mark returned to his truck to get his tools, and Leslie

pushed open her office door. Unfortunately, the stacks of files, reports, and newspapers hadn't spontaneously combusted.

In only three weeks, the new tax season would take off. If she did some marketing, remodeling, and updating, she could turn the profit margin for this branch completely around. Showing that kind of improvement would surely move her to a bigger branch, or the main office, or at least an office closer to the city.

Leslie looked around her office. The walls were the color of cigarette smoke, and the furniture had been manufactured in 1975. Dusty harvest gold and olive green covered every Formica and fabric surface. She imagined that the surfaces hidden by stacks of paper were in much the same degree of ugliness.

She grabbed the phone book and flipped to the ten pages of yellow in the back. Pausing on the *Cs,* she scanned the list for construction companies. There were four. Well, at least she wouldn't have to review a lot of estimates. She dialed the first number. The phone rang three times, and then a computerized voice answered, saying, "Please leave your message." The voice was followed by several beeps, and then the call disconnected.

Leslie punched in the second number and was greeted with a similar message. She waited through the series of beeps. After the last one, she started to leave her name and contact information but was cut off by the dial tone.

Big Bubba's Demolition and Construction was next on the list. That demolition was listed before construction was cause for concern, but she dialed the number any-way. She only had two names left.

"Yello," a gruff voice answered on the second ring.

Leslie hadn't expected anyone to answer, so it took a second to gather her thoughts for a conversation.

"Yello," the voice said again. "Hello? Junior, you'd better not be crank calling me again."

"No. I'm sorry." She paused. "I'm Leslie Knotts, call-ing from Hanston and Boyd. I'd like to get an estimate on having some work done at my office."

"Huh." A slurpy sound came across the phone line, and Leslie suspected that the man had almost lost his chaw.

"What kinda trailer is it?"

"Trailer? It's not a trailer. It's an office in a strip mall."

"Uh. We only do trailers. We rip 'em down and sell the scrap metal."

"Can you at least come out and look at this job?" Leslie persisted.

"No, sir—I mean, ma'am. We's only do trailers." And he hung up the phone.

Leslie pulled the receiver away from her ear.

"Good-bye to you, too."

She was down to the last name on the list. Reluctantly, she dialed the number. This time the rings were inter-rupted by the nasal operator voice informing her the number had been disconnected.

She slammed the phone down. There was only one company still in business and answering their phone, and they didn't do construction.

This was Chuck's fault. She wasn't exactly sure how, but it felt better to blame him. In fact, everything that happened to her here was his fault, including her lock's sticking this morning and her attraction to Mark. She was here because of Chuck, so it was his fault.

Just as she contemplated whipping every troll snow-globe paperweight on her desk at the wall, the door swung open.

"Leslie." Mark poked his head through the opening. "I've got the pipe fixed and new ceiling tiles in. Let me know if you need anything else."

"Thanks, Mark," she said absently, lifting one of the paperweights in her hand. "Wait!" she called after him, dropping the paperweight onto the desk. The iridescent glitter swirled around the NASCAR troll's head.

Mark stuck his head back through the doorway.

"What company do you work for? I heard you had four other jobs."

"I don't. I mean, just one, my own. I'm trying to get my own business going."

"Do you do more than leaky pipes?"

Mark leaned against the doorjamb, allowing the office door to swing wide open.

"I've done a lot of home projects. Room remodels, repairs. That kind of thing."

"Do you do offices?" Excitement startled bubbling through her again.

"Not yet."

Leslie slouched back in her seat. Having the office re-modeled would go a long way toward reaching new cus-tomers, but now it wouldn't happen.

"Thanks anyway." She plunked her head onto her desk.

"What'd you have in mind?"

"I have no idea."

Mark laughed. "You seem awfully disappointed for 'no idea.'"

"This place needs an updated look. It reminds me of my grandmother's kitchen, with all the olive green and dark paneling. I think I could draw new clients if it wasn't so ugly."

"I'm not an interior decorator," Mark warned.

"I know. I need to take down the paneling. Hang dry-wall. Paint."

"Gotcha." Mark nodded, his gaze creeping along the walls of the office. "You want to take a walk with me and point out what you want? Then I'll come up with a price."

Leslie bounced out of her seat. "That would be fantastic." She gave him a quick hug, noticing the hardness of the muscles under his sweatshirt. She felt herself relaxing against his warmth. She pulled away when she felt his unshaven jaw brush her cheek.

"Let's start with the reception area." She hurried down the hallway, desperate for some space. What was she thinking? Totally inappropriate behavior, she scolded. He was her employee. It had to be long-term aftereffects of the punch. Those Library Ladies must have laced it with a time-release aphrodisiac. She entered the main office, conscious of Mark's boots echoing behind her.

"What would you like to do?" Mark asked, pulling a notebook and a flat carpenter's pencil from his pocket.

Leslie scanned the room and shrugged. It was ugly and dark and decidedly uninviting.

"The paneling definitely needs to go, as well as the

carpet." She rolled the desk chair aside, and carpet bubbled under the casters.

"How about changing the shape of the room?" Mark asked. He thumped his fist against a wall. "These are partitions and can be rearranged."

"How?"

"You could tear them down and add more seating along this wall." He unclipped a retractable tape measure from his belt and measured the wall. "It would add another five feet along this wall."

"It'd give us room for a play area. People could bring their kids. Convenience is important, especially during tax season."

Pictures formed in Leslie's mind. "If I moved the receptionist's desk closer to the door, it'd also open the seating area up. I could do a couple of different groupings of chairs." Leslie tapped a finger against her lip, studying the current layout.

Mark jotted measurements in his notebook.

"I'm going to need more electrical outlets. Data connections, too."

"You're certainly jumping into the manager's job. I don't think this place has been refurbished since the early eighties."

"It's a means to an end," she said, examining the ceiling tiles.

"How's that?" Mark tucked his pencil behind one ear.

"If I improve sales here, I'll likely get a real promotion."

Mark bent over an electrical socket. "These aren't grounded. We'll need an electrician to check them out."

"Can't you fix them?"

"No. I took an electrical course but couldn't pass the exams." Mark scratched the back of his head. "I'm not certified."

"Why not?" Leslie asked, suddenly feeling worried. If the walls fell on someone, headquarters would "notice" her with a pink slip.

"Color-blind." He tapped his temple. "I kept crossing the red and green wires. I can figure them out, but I wouldn't want to chance getting the wires mixed up on a commercial project."

"We'll hire an electrician, then. When would you be able to start?"

Mark flipped a couple pages of his notebook. "I'll have to run the numbers and get back to you with an estimate. Do you want to do anything with the other rooms?"

Leslie studied the aging paneling. "Just my office and the bathrooms. They'll have the most impact on sales."

"How's that?" Mark asked.

"People'll come in to see what we've done. If it looks good and the prices are reasonable, they'll tell their friends. Word of mouth is your best marketing tool."

"You have to build a good reputation."

"This could help your business, too. Put a sign in the window, so people know who's doing the remodeling. I do need this project done pretty quickly."

"How quickly?" Mark shoved his notebook into a back pocket.

"February first."

"It's tight, but I can do it. I don't have much else going on." He flashed a grin.

"It's only a couple of weeks, isn't it?" She smoothed her hair back. "If all goes well, I could be back in the city by May."

"Eager to get out of here, huh?"

"If I can remind headquarters I still exist and show my value to the company, they'll give me a real promotion." Leslie crossed her arms across her chest.

"A branch manager sounds like a pretty good job to me."

Leslie sighed. "This wasn't a promotion. It was backstabbing by someone I thought was my friend. I want to be a CEO, not a branch manager. I was so close."

Tears threatened, but she willed them away. CEOs didn't cry, and she wouldn't either.

Chapter Six

Leslie dashed for the ringing phone.

"Hanston and Boyd Accounting, how may I help you?" she panted into the receiver.

A deep voice laughed. "You're so busy, you're out of breath? I find that hard to believe."

"What is it, Chuck?" She glanced at her watch. Her morning was passing much move slowly than she'd expected. She'd tackled the paperwork in the women's bathroom, hoping to create space to move the older files out of her office. Tax returns from 1985 and before stuffed every available inch of the putty-colored file cabinets. She hated to think how old the files in the rest of the building were. They didn't need to keep records back that far.

"What, no, 'Hey, baby, how are ya?' "

"I think we've established that while you may be several other people's 'baby,' you are not mine." She kept a few papers, but mostly she fed the shredder. The blades were already dull. She'd need to order new ones. She'd ask Mark about it. That'd be easier than another fiasco with the telephone book.

"That hurts, Leslie."

"It should." Maybe she should set the place on fire. The files crumpled in her fingers. It would save her the trouble of going through all of this garbage.

There was silence at the other end of the line.

"Why are you calling, Chuck?" she asked, grimacing at the streaks of dust across the sleeves of her cream silk blouse. She hoped Carterville had a good dry cleaner. Her wardrobe was going to need it.

"I wanted to see how you were doing."

"I'm fine. Leave me alone. Stop calling." Her stomach growled. There was a cute Chinese buffet a couple of doors down. She could get takeout and keep sorting while she ate. She hated going to a restaurant by herself.

"Leslie." His voice dropped to a whisper. "There's something you should know. There's a lot of rumors."

She imagined him crouching over his phone. "I'm not interested in gossip."

"It's not gossip. There are consultants here, looking at reports, analyzing, interviewing. Ms. Boyd's in meetings all the time. Mr. Hanston must be, too. I haven't seen him."

"Are we getting audited?"

"No one will say who they are, but some of the rumors are about restructuring."

"Is that all? You've kissed enough behinds to keep your job. I'm at a branch in Podunkville, so any restructuring at the central office won't include me."

"That's the thing. This isn't just headquarters. It's the whole company. All the branches, too."

Leslie frowned at the phone. "You're giving me a heads-up?"

This sounded like the friend Chuck had been when she first started, willing to help her out. Before she understood his ulterior motives.

"Yeah." He coughed. "Just be ready."

"When are they coming?"

"Not sure. Everything's pretty hush-hush."

"How do you know so much?"

"They've let me in on a couple of meetings."

"Meaning you've eavesdropped." Leslie shuffled papers on her desk to find the phone book. She was definitely going to work through lunch today.

"No. I've actually sat in on a couple of meetings. They asked about some of the clients I've worked with."

"So your job is safe." He was calling to rub it in. *Figures*.

"No one is safe, babe. I wanted to remind you to keep private things private."

Finally, the real reason for his call.

"I doubt it'd do me any good to tell them."

Leslie dropped the phone into its cradle and sighed. Her stomach grumbled again. She definitely needed takeout now, because she had to spend every waking minute getting this place shipshape before the consultants came.

"Leslie, is that you?" Minnie called from the kitchen. "I've got dinner all ready."

Leslie stopped in the entryway, her briefcase strap

sliding off her shoulder. All she wanted was a long, hot shower to work some of the aches out of her body. Standing in heels all day made everything ache. She'd have to drag a chair into that bathroom tomorrow.

"Hey, Minnie," she called. "I'm going to take a shower and go to bed." Running a hand over her hair, she realized it was coated with dust and cobwebs. Even her black pants had taken on a dusty sheen. Maybe a long, soaking bath would be a better idea.

Minnie came out of the kitchen, drying her hands on a lined towel. "You can't skip dinner. I'll send up a tray."

Leslie thanked her. "I'll let you know when I'm done with my shower." She climbed the stairs, wishing Minnie would leave her alone. Minnie was like a second mother—in all the bad ways. Minnie nagged her to eat, commented on how much she worked, and worried about how little she slept. At least she hadn't tried to rearrange Leslie's hair.

Leslie let herself into her room and went directly to the shower. She twisted the dial to hot. Steamy water cascaded from the multiple showerheads. She stripped off her clothes, dropping them on the floor in a dusty pile. The warm water massaged her sore muscles and washed away the dust and the cobwebs. She sighed in relaxation.

The auditors were coming, but she had a few weeks. A small office should be a low priority on their list. She'd have plenty of time to get the office cleaned up, remodeled, and prepared for the next season. Maybe the place would be bustling with new customers when the consultants finally arrived.

She stepped out of the shower feeling more calm and confident. She would have an opportunity to prove herself just as the tax season was starting. She could be back at headquarters within six months. The consultants would see the turnaround of the branch and recommend her for a promotion. She might even be Chuck's boss.

Wrapping her towel around her chest and tucking in the edge, she plopped onto the bed. Shaking out her hair, she finger-combed the tangles.

Dinner.

Now she was hungry. She called Minnie. Minnie said she could bring a tray up, but Leslie told her she'd come down to the kitchen in a few minutes.

Leslie had barely tugged open the top drawer of her dresser when a knock sounded at her door. She hurried to open it, sure Minnie was carrying a heavy tray.

"I told you I'd be down in a minute. You didn't have to carry a tray up—"

But Minnie wasn't standing in the doorway with a tray of food.

Mark was.

Leslie clutched her towel, holding the tucked edges together. What was he doing here, carrying her dinner? Was he working here now, too? Why had she opened the door? Why hadn't she said 'just a minute' and pulled on the panties she was digging for. Panties? She glanced at her hands. Thankfully, they only held her towel. She wasn't waving her underwear at him, too.

Her whole body blushed as his gaze traveled over her. His eyes traced every inch of her bare skin. Finally, mercifully, he turned his face away from her.

"I'm sorry. I should have announced myself." His dimples deepened when he grinned. He at least had the decency to look sheepish.

"I didn't know you were here at the bed-and-breakfast. I thought Minnie was at the door. I told her I would be down in a few minutes. I was wondering why she came up. She didn't have to send you up." Leslie realized she was rambling. "I was getting dressed, and then I'd be on my way down," she finished slowly. Leslie slipped behind the door while she was talking and peeked around the edge. The towel covered her from chest to knees, but knowing there was nothing underneath it made her feel naked. She ran a tentative hand across her hair, trying to smooth down the remaining tangles.

"Where should I put this?" Mark asked, lifting the tray.

"Over on the table." Leslie opened the door farther, shielding her body behind it. Her briefcase sat on the only table in the room. There were two frail-looking chairs on either side of it. She debated whether to move her briefcase for him, but that meant leaving the protection of her door.

Mark easily balanced the tray and moved her briefcase to the floor. He deposited the tray on the table and turned around. "I didn't mean to surprise you. Minnie claimed her back was hurting and she couldn't carry the tray. I'm scraping wallpaper in the back bedroom, and Minnie said she wouldn't feed me unless I did her a favor."

"I told Minnie I was coming down." Leslie shrugged her shoulders as he walked toward the door. "I don't know why she sent you up."

"Enjoy your dinner," he said, walking through the doorway.

Leslie was closing the door as he walked out when he stopped and muttered something. When he turned back to her, she was staring into his bright blue eyes. Leslie's breath caught.

He contemplated her, his eyes narrowed. "You haven't been to the Ladies' Night Out, have you?"

Leslie blinked. "Last Friday."

"I thought so." He rolled his eyes and shook his head. "Don't they ever let up? Just a heads-up. I've been their target since last summer." He rubbed a hand through his hair. "I don't know how I fell for this again."

"They did mention you. Their only failure. But there was some dispute among the women about that," Leslie said, trying to smile even though her heart pounded in her chest. He was so close, she could smell the scent of sawdust clinging to his clothing.

Mark sighed. "I think they've set their sights on you as well."

"Me?" Leslie released her grip on the door and stepped away. She clutched her towel. No matter how tightly the edge was tucked against her breast, she wasn't taking a chance it would fall. "This is how they do it? Embarrass the heck out of someone? I expected some sort of black magic." She laughed. "How many naked women have you walked in on?"

"You're the first naked one." He glanced down, then quickly raised his eyes back to her face. "I mean, almost naked." He scratched the back of his neck. "Not that

I noticed. I mean . . ." He muttered something Leslie couldn't make out.

She knew he'd looked. Head to toe, she'd felt every millisecond of it.

"Minnie knew I was taking a shower." She fumbled for something to say. "Then I was coming downstairs."

"She hoped you'd be fresh from your shower and all warm and rosy, and I'd be overcome by your relaxed beauty. Or she wanted me to walk in on you naked." He coughed and shoved his hands into his pockets. "Minnie has a weird sense of romance."

Leslie knew she should thank him and let him go. Put them both out of their misery. She was warm and rosy, but it had nothing to do with being freshly scrubbed. Mark hadn't moved. She fidgeted with the edge of her towel and then realized that Mark's eyes were locked on her hand. Which was in front of her chest.

"Would you like to join me?" she blurted out. "For dinner, I mean."

Who was controlling her tongue? She wanted to get out of this embarrassing situation, but she couldn't take the invitation back. When he hesitated, she added, "I'll put on some clothes."

She kicked herself again. She wanted him to decline. She wasn't supposed to make it easier to say yes.

He laughed. "Sure. Do you want me to wait in the hall?"

"I'll change in the bathroom." She tugged a pair of linen pants off a hanger, grabbed a cashmere sweater out of the dresser, and snatched underwear out of the still-open drawer as she scurried past. She shut the bathroom door as her towel started to slip. "I'll be right back."

Mark coughed. "I don't know why they've been picking on me. I always fall for it, too. For the record, I didn't hesitate because of your towel. I didn't want Minnie jumping to her obvious conclusions. She's watching from the bottom of the stairs and is already on the phone with Yvonne."

Leslie combed her hair and twisted it into a bun at the base of her neck. As she jabbed each pin into her hair, she felt more like herself. She could get through this without seeming like a complete nitwit. She smoothed the fold marks out of her pants and checked herself in the mirror. She looked put together now. She grabbed a pair of gold hoop earrings off the countertop and put them on. Her stomach growled again, reminding her of the food on the other side of the door.

She emerged from the bathroom as Mark removed the plates from the tray and arranged them on the small table. He had moved the two straight-backed chairs in the room to the sides of the table. Neither chair looked as if it was meant to support the weight of more than a toddler, but these were the only chairs that could be moved to the table. She'd stacked a bunch of stuff on the only upholstered chair. Mark seemed less than surprised that there two plates and enough food to feed a horse.

"It looks as if Minnie expected you to stay." Leslie laughed. She took a seat on one of the chairs. The wooden joints creaked a little but then were quiet. "I could never eat all this food. Well, maybe all the chocolate pudding.

Yum." Plates were piled with fried chicken, mashed potatoes, honey buns, and chocolate pudding.

Mark sat down in the other chair. It also creaked but more loudly. He winced.

"If I ate even half of this on a regular basis, I'd need bigger pants." Leslie tore a piece of breading off the chicken. "Delicious. Minnie sure can cook."

"She's about the best cook I know," Mark agreed, taking a bite of buttered honey bun.

Leslie curled her legs under her and nibbled the chicken. "How many times have the Library Ladies set you up?"

Mark reached for a piece of chicken. "This makes seven."

"Seven?" Leslie nearly choked on her food. "I only heard about one."

"The crazy one?" Mark dipped the bun in gravy. "That's the only one they apologize for."

"Were the others as bad?" Leslie grimaced and buttered her own honey bun.

Mark dragged his fork through his mashed potatoes. "No. The Ladies don't know when to stop. Sure, it was funny it first, but the women kept getting stranger. I think the Ladies got less particular. I don't get why they don't trust me to find someone on my own. Some of the women were attractive but not my type."

Leslie knew she shouldn't care, but she asked anyway. "What is your type?"

"Normal. Average. Everyday all-American girl." He shrugged. "If that's a type."

Leslie arched an eyebrow. "It sounds like a Hooters waitress to me."

Mark grinned. "But I can't tell you that."

"Ah." Leslie nodded and smiled. "The Library Ladies can't find blond and big boobs for you in small-town America?"

"The closest they've gotten is peroxide." Mark scooped more mashed potatoes onto his plate.

"I should be appalled. You just told me you're only attracted to Pamela Anderson wannabes. It's what's disgusting about men. They only care about what's on the surface."

"At least I was honest. It's not all I care about, but it's a place to start."

"Refreshing," she said sarcastically. She chucked a piece of bread across the table at him, feeling more self-conscious about her brown hair and decidedly small chest.

"I'm not playing along with their game," said Mark.

"I don't exactly fit your description of an all-American girl," she replied flatly. She really shouldn't be disappointed. She wasn't looking for anything, and she worked with him. If it fell apart, it'd be awkward. She'd been down that path before, and it had done nothing for her career. Or her self-esteem, for that matter. The branch in Carterville was the worst possible transfer, but the betrayal by Chuck had been much worse. They'd watched out for each other in the office, keeping each other aware of office politics. And he'd stabbed her in the back. Sending her here to save his own behind.

"I'm saying I'm not trying to entrap you or anything.

The Library Ladies think that they have to do the looking for me."

"You haven't been attracted to any of the other women?" she asked, finding it hard to believe a man could be set up with seven women and not find any of them attractive. From her experience, men found breathing attractive.

"They weren't my type," he repeated.

"You couldn't get past the peroxide and the Wonderbra?"

"Usually I saw the setup before it got that far. It wasn't like a relationship actually started."

"Then what happened with the crazy one? I thought you went on at least one real date with her."

"She did have a Wonderbra." He stabbed a spoon into a cup of pudding.

"Hey!" She slapped his wrist with her fork. She wasn't giving up the chocolate. "That's the bigger pudding. I've been looking forward to that chocolate since you brought it in."

"You said it'd make you fat," he said, picking up the cup and leaning back in his seat.

"If I ate it on a regular basis. Now drop it."

"I thought I was doing you a favor."

"Are you saying I'm fat?"

"You may have gotten me to say I like blonds with big breasts, but I'm not even going to touch that one." He grudgingly handed her the pudding.

Leslie took a triumphant scoop and slowly licked off the spoon. Pure heaven. "I'm sure that should be taken as an insult, but this is so good, I don't even care."

"You're not fat." He reached for the other cup of pudding.

"Thank you. I'm glad you fell for that." Leslie licked another spoonful of pudding.

"Devious." He narrowed his eyes. "How can I be sure you aren't in on the Library Ladies' plot? It wouldn't be the first time." He shook his spoon at her.

"I can assure you, the last thing I am looking for is a husband, a commitment, or even a date. And I always answer the door of my hotel room wearing a towel, so don't think you got a special show." She waved her spoon like a scolding finger.

"That's what every woman says when asked. Well, except the towel thing." Scrunching up his forehead, he contemplated his empty pudding cup.

"You already said I failed. Brown is my natural color, and Wonderbras still need something to push up to be effective."

"You invited me in, and you licked chocolate seductively off your spoon." He looked at her skeptically.

Licking seductively? Her seducing him? Leslie dropped her spoon into the empty cup and set them on the table. The spoon clattered against a glass. She'd never seduced anyone. Seduction required a level of surrender she didn't think she was capable of. She pressed her cool fingers to her burning cheeks. She needed to stop thinking this way.

"It could be an elaborate ploy to make me forget all about my Pamela Anderson fantasies."

Leslie snorted. "Now, that thought could induce vomiting. I may never recover."

"What?" Mark held his hands up and leaned back in

his chair. It creaked threateningly. He glanced down at the legs.

"You owe me." She crossed her arms in front of her chest.

"For what?"

Leslie held a hand up and checked things off by raising her fingers.

"You saw me naked."

"You were decently covered."

"Nevertheless." She shook her head. "You called me fat."

"You provoked me, and I apologized already."

"And finally, you put the words *Pamela Anderson* and *fantasy* into the same sentence." She shuddered. "Anyway, you owe me."

He studied her, then held up his hands. "I surrender. What do you want?"

"I need to relax, and since there's nothing good on TV, I want to be entertained."

"I don't do stripteases." He laughed.

"Pity." Leslie forced herself to breathe normally and rolled her eyes. That would be more interesting than a Hallmark movie. But he didn't need to know she found the idea appealing. She needed more chocolate pudding. "I want to hear about all the almost dates the Library Ladies tried."

"That could take some time. Do you have a towel?"

"Why?" Leslie asked, stacking the dishes back on the tray.

"If I sit on that chair any longer, I'm going to break it. I don't want to get your bed dusty. I cleaned most of the wallpaper scraps off, but there may be some clinging to my shirt." He twisted his neck to check over his shoulder. He pulled some of the pillows off the bed and stacked the remaining ones into a mountain on one side.

"My bed? What are you doing?" she gasped.

"There isn't another place to sit." He crossed his arms over his chest. "Do you want to hear the stories or not?"

"There is a perfectly sturdy chair right there." She gestured to the rather antique-looking purple armchair on which she had piled the bras and stockings she'd rinsed out the previous night. She snatched a shirt from the top of the bureau and tossed it over the pile. Now he'd seen her almost naked *and* seen her underwear. How else could she humiliate herself in his presence? At least the lacy Victoria's Secret bra was on top. "Right. Get off my bed. You can lie on the floor. I want to sit on my bed."

He gestured to the purple-encased queen-size bed. "There is plenty of room for both of us." He went into the bathroom and yanked a clean towel out of the basket by the tub. After spreading it across one side of the bed, he rearranged the pile of pillows.

"What are you doing?" she asked as he lay down on his back and stretched his arms above his head.

"Getting comfortable. I have several stories to tell, and it feels like something I should lie down for. Like I'm in therapy." He punched a pillow and balled it behind his head. "Perfect."

"Couldn't you find another chair or something?" Leslie chewed her lower lip. "From another room?"

Mark leaned back and put his hands behind his head. "There's room for both of us here." He patted the purple comforter next to him. "Do you want to hear the stories or not?"

She looked at him skeptically.

"If I had ulterior motives, don't you think I'd have acted on them when you answered the door naked?" He raised his eyebrows at her.

"Yeah. I get it." That was a kick to her ego. She climbed onto the bed and used the remaining pillows for her own headrest. She left a full twelve inches between them. "Girlfriend number one?"

"They weren't girlfriends. They were setups. I wouldn't even call them dates."

"Whatever. Setup number one." She held her hands out as if introducing him. After all this finagling to get him to tell the stories, they'd better be good.

"It was at my friend Tom's wedding. I was the best man, and the maid of honor was available."

"Everyone has one of those stories. Even I have one of those stories. This had better improve." Leslie pulled one of the pillows into her lap and started picking at the lace.

"Will you let me tell it?" He rolled his eyes. "It was one of those theme weddings. Tom is a better man than I am for putting up with it all."

"Wait." Leslie sat up and turned toward him. "Did he marry Wendy?" At Mark's nod, she said, "I heard about that. You're lucky it wasn't the bride's grandmother."

"Good point." He rolled to his side and propped himself on his elbow. "Were you like that as a brides-maid?"

"Of course not." She scowled at him. "I did have a groomsman vomit on my dyed-to-match teal shoes."

"I hope you didn't keep them."

"Pitched 'em before I left the reception. Would've tossed the dress, too, but I couldn't throw a two-hundred-dollar dress into the garbage, no matter how ugly it was."

Mark sat up and turned to punch the pillows into a better shape. "Did you have a date?"

"What? No. Why?" They were discussing his dating life, not hers.

"Curious."

"So, the next one. What was it like?"

Mark grabbed the lace-edged pillows and tossed them to the floor. "The lace scratches. What do they make it out of? Straw?" He flopped back and sighed. "The second one was a week later. Some girl's car broke down in front of Yvonne's. Could I come and give her a ride into town?" He mimicked Yvonne's Kentucky accent.

"The damsel in distress. I've heard of that one." Leslie rolled onto her side to face Mark. "These women have ingenuity. I'd better watch out. I don't want all the single men in town hunting me down. Bringing me dinner when I'm naked." She laughed.

"That's where I have the advantage. They have to search for out-of-town women for me. I've been set up with all the women in town under the age of forty."

"All of them?"

Mark drew little hash marks with his finger in the air. "Yep. All of them. It's a small town."

"I can't believe I'm with the most eligible bachelor of Carterville."

"I grew up here. They've had a lot of time to hassle me. Considering how many of them I've actually gone out with, I wouldn't describe myself as the George Clooney of Carterville." He winked.

Leslie gave him a wry grin.

"How many *men* do I have to worry about? I have work to do at the office, and I don't want to have men crawling all over themselves for the chance to see me open my door in a towel."

"The view would be worth it," Mark mused aloud. "Unfortunately for you, there's quite a few. Lisa keeps a folder of profiles. She's offered to help me several times."

"Why didn't you take her up on it? You could drag out the process. Let the Library Ladies think they were finally having some success."

"It wouldn't work that way. They wouldn't be content. If they don't see adequate progress, they interfere more. You should have seen Tom before he proposed to Wendy. The Ladies drove him nuts. I don't want that to happen to me."

"Why don't they give up?" Leslie asked.

"They don't think any single person should be alone. They think because I'm not dating, I'm not looking."

"Are you looking?" Not that she was personally interested in his answer, of course. She was making conversation.

"When I find the right one, I'll ask her out. It's as simple as that. I don't need their help."

"How will you know if she's the right one? Will fireworks explode around her?"

He chuckled. "Probably not, but I'll know. I need to get my construction company off the ground. Once it's running smoothly, then maybe . . ."

"I'm with you there. If the phone ever rings at the office, I need it to be a legitimate customer—unless it's Hugh Jackman. Then I'd reconsider."

"Sorry, but I think he's married." Mark sat up and tugged his sweatshirt over his head. "Are you hot? I'm roasting here. Minnie's been messing with the furnace again." He dropped the shirt to the floor next to the bed and pulled his T-shirt back into place, but not before Leslie got an up-close view of his sculpted abdominal muscles.

Leslie agreed about the warmth but inwardly doubted it had anything to do with the thermostat. "Would any of these Carterville guys be worth it? I don't think there's a way for me to get out of this."

Mark made a face. "There's a couple of nice guys, I guess. If you don't have any objections to hygiene issues."

Leslie shuddered. "Great." She chewed her lower lip. "If they don't believe this"—she gestured between them—"is working, they'll send the rest of the town after me. I could gain some customers for the tax service, but I don't need a bunch of smelly guys hovering around me. I need to get the office remodeled and get my promotion. Consultants are evaluating the company and will be visiting the branches soon."

"When?"

"They just show up." She shook her head. "This is the smallest branch, so it's low priority. I figure I have at least a month."

"If I start demolition tomorrow, we can have it finished by the time they arrive."

"Fantastic."

"It's an optimistic estimate. Everything'd have to go smoothly."

But Leslie ignored him. "I'll get a real promotion and be able to move back to the city." And get on with her climb up the corporate ladder. She would be a CEO someday.

"You know," Mark said slowly, "we may have a solution to our problem with the Ladies."

"What's that?" Leslie asked, sitting up.

"We could trick them at their own game. Let them think their plan worked."

"Go on."

"It'd be perfect, actually. I'll be at your office working on the remodel. We can let them think there's more going on."

"More going on?" Leslie wasn't sure what he meant by that. Some ideas rushed into her mind.

"We can let them know we're having lunch together. Spending a lot of time together, working on this big project. That should keep them happy for a while."

"You'll be saved from damsels in distress, and I'll be saved from untimely dinner deliveries. And hygiene issues. They'll believe their plan worked with no other evidence?"

"I think they'll be happy enough if I am wherever you are. They can read volumes into any gesture. We may have to do some acting occasionally, but I can handle it if you can."

"Acting?" Images and sensations flew into her mind. She took a deep breath to calm the pounding of her heart. She supposed she could endure that. "Agreed." She held out her hand, and Mark shook it.

"Should we practice this first?" he asked, leaning toward her, his gaze drifting over her face.

"Practice?" Her whole body froze in anticipation. "Like pet names?"

Mark cleared his throat. "I had something else in mind." His blue eyes stared at her intently.

Leslie stopped breathing. She couldn't get herself to agree. The offer was more tempting than chocolate pudding, but she didn't think she could trust herself. "We'll manage if we need to," she said, amazed at how steady her voice sounded.

Mark nodded and checked his watch. "I should be going. I've got a long day of work ahead of me." He sat up on the bed and reached for his sweatshirt.

She wasn't sure, but she thought he might be disappointed.

Let the charade begin.

Chapter Seven

Mark wedged the flat edge of his crowbar behind the last piece of paneling. A quick jerk on the bar freed it from the wall and sent it tumbling to the floor. A cloud of dust hovered in the air. In three days the room had changed from a dated office to a pile of debris. He'd torn down everything from the dropped ceilings to the paneling and thrown them into a giant pile. He leaned the crowbar against the wall and sat down on the floor. Only the carpet was left. When he was done ripping out the old stuff, he could start on what he really enjoyed: rebuilding. Well, he could as soon as he carted all this junk to the Dumpster outside.

He liked working with Leslie. She was encouraging and understanding about the noise and the mess. Other customers complained about the noise of the saws or the never-ending dust, and it was frustrating because neither one was avoidable.

He caught Leslie watching him work a couple of times. He pretended not to see her and kept working, willing himself to move as if he was oblivious to her presence. He couldn't remember what he was planning to do next when her eyes were on him. He hoped she didn't think he was lazy when she saw him wander aimlessly for a moment or two.

They had lunch together every day. He admired the glow in her eyes when she talked about her dreams. Her determination was so strong. It was hard to imagine anyone more determined or driven to succeed. He caught himself forgetting what she was saying as he watched the excitement grow in her face and the movement of her lips.

Usually then his thoughts strayed completely. Then he reminded himself that Leslie was not his fantasy and they were just spending time together to keep Minnie off their backs.

The Library Ladies nibbled at the bait, but they had yet to swallow it completely. They hadn't called him to jump-start any cars, but Minnie was still less than subtle about Leslie whenever he worked at the bed-and-breakfast. He might have to do something else to convince them.

"Caught you sitting down on the job again," Leslie joked from her office. She leaned against the doorway, surveying the room and the debris pile in the middle of the floor. "It's an improvement with the paneling gone."

"It'll look better after I rip out the carpet."

Leslie nodded. She'd left her suit jacket in her office and was wearing one of those silky blouses. A tight black skirt curved around her hips. Her hair was pulled back into a tight twist, but strands escaped and floated softly around her face.

Those floating tendrils had him itching to intertwine his fingers in her hair. The thought surprised him, given his penchant for shapely blonds. But she looked relaxed, tired, and happy, and he found that attractive.

"I'm going to get something for lunch. You want anything?" she asked.

"Where are you going?"

"Bart's Sandwich Shop. I could bring back a pizza meal deal."

"Sounds good. I'm going to see what's under this carpet." He pushed himself off the floor and stood up. He could ask her about attending Bryce's figure-eight race while they were eating lunch.

Leslie waited in line at the counter as Bart chatted briefly with each customer. Bart wore a paper sailor hat and a soiled apron over an overstretched T-shirt. The man in front of her hadn't even placed an order. Bart brought him a sandwich box and a Coke and jotted the price on a notepad next to the cash register. The man must come here every day.

Leslie told Bart her order.

"That's an awful lot for a little thing like you," Bart said, making a note on his pad. "We'll get some meat on those bones yet."

Leslie smiled thinly. Why was everyone in this town so nosy? The Library Ladies seemed to be the rule rather than the exception. "I'm splitting lunch with Mark today."

"Oh, I see." Bart winked at her. He handed her a

receipt. "He's such a nice young man. I'll bring your food right out."

"Thanks." Leslie stuffed the receipt into her purse and stepped away from the counter before Bart could make another comment about her and Mark or her weight.

Most of the tables were crowded with people munching on Bart's famous subs or a slice of his pizza. The dining room was surrounded by plate glass windows, but near the counter were several pictures of Bart and his family eating pizza or holding the largest submarine sandwiches she'd ever seen.

"Leslie!" Someone called her name.

Leslie turned to see Yvonne, Dinah, and Betty crowded around a table littered with sandwich wrappers, paper cups, and the lettuce remains of three sandwiches. Yvonne waved her over.

There's no escaping them. Leslie sighed. She slung her purse over her shoulder and headed for their table.

"We can make room, if you need a place to sit." Betty and Dinah were already scooting their chairs aside to make room.

"Oh. That's all right. I'm getting takeout. Mark's waiting."

Three sets of eyebrows rose. Three sets of eyes shared intrigued glances.

Mark was right. The whole thing with dinner the other night had been planned. If these three weren't in on it from the beginning, they certainly knew about it now.

"He's in the middle of ripping the carpeting out and didn't want to stop. I said I'd pick something up."

The three ladies looked at one another and then back at her.

"It must be nice to have him around all day." Dinah smiled.

"I don't get to see him much." *Except for the times I catch myself gazing out my doorway.* She needed to stop that. And she certainly couldn't let them know about it. "We're working in two different areas of the building."

The three ladies exchanged looks again. Leslie guessed they weren't happy with her answer. Mark had thought the Library Ladies would be content knowing they were together all day, but Leslie had dispelled that idea. *Oops.*

"What do you think of him?" Betty asked, picking up the lettuce pieces on the table and dropping them into her napkin.

I think I'm falling in love, was on the tip of her tongue, but she couldn't admit that. Instead Leslie said, "He's nice."

"Don't you think he's cute?" asked Yvonne, digging through her purse for a comb and smoothing her iron gray curls. "I could just pinch his cheeks."

Leslie hoped for Mark's sake that Yvonne meant the ones on his face.

"He deserves someone special," Dinah added.

"He seems to be a hard worker. I never thought he'd have so much of the junk torn out so quickly," Leslie added. "I've really been impressed.

"You mean he's working on the building? I thought he was answering the phone," said Betty.

"I need him for the construction more. The office needs an update."

The women nodded in agreement.

"It's so nice of you to give him a chance. He's trying to get his business off the ground, but it takes a while."

"So you guys don't get to talk much, then?"

This is what Mark meant about putting on a show. It was going to be harder than she thought. She was in accounting, for goodness' sake. Hard numbers couldn't be anything other than what they were. She had no talent for spinning and twisting the facts.

"I do look forward to our lunches together." She smiled in what she hoped was a decent Scarlett O'Hara impression. And, truthfully, she did. Mark helped her keep everything in perspective. He calmed her anxiety about the consultants and filled her with optimism about their project. She liked referring to the remodel as "theirs." Hers and Mark's.

The Library Ladies seemed somewhat relieved.

Luckily, Bart brought her order out to her right then. She waved to the Ladies and hurried out the door.

Mark stabbed his utility knife into the edge of the carpet and pulled. The carpet tore away from the wall. Mark jerked it back, tearing the top layer of carpet away from the floor. Beneath, the almost nonexistent layer of padding clung alternately to the back of the carpet and to the floor. He groaned. He was going to have to find an industrial adhesive remover and spend hours scraping. He continued ripping the top layer of carpet away and tossing the pieces into the debris pile.

The door chimed as Mark retracted the blade on his knife and dropped it into his pocket. He kicked a roll of carpet toward the pile.

"Excuse me, are you the manager, Leslie Knotts?" a nasal voice asked from the doorway.

Mark looked up to see two men in expensive business suits. He guessed they would be able to light a room with a single candle and the reflection off their bald heads. He saw their frown lines deepen as they surveyed him, the deconstructed room, and the giant pile of splintered wood and carpet pieces.

"No." Mark stepped forward, holding out his hand. "I'm the project manager for the remodel."

"I see," Uptight Man A said, pursing his lips and ignoring Mark's outstretched hand.

Mark waited for them to introduce themselves. When they said nothing, he supplied, "Ms. Knotts went to pick up lunch. She'll be back any minute now."

Uptight Man B looked at Uptight Man A with a look of frustration. Uptight Man A shrugged.

"We're with Van Haitsma Consulting. Is there somewhere else we can wait for her?" Uptight Man A asked. His gaze shifted about the room.

Uptight Man B sneezed.

Mark decided not to point out the two plastic chairs upended in the pile and led them down the hall to Leslie's office. He pushed the door open and stifled a groan. He had forgotten how much paper was stacked in there.

The two men looked around, and Mark was sure their frown lines became permanent. Leslie would not be happy about this, but there wasn't any other place. He didn't think taking them to the break room would help Leslie's cause.

"The mess is from the previous manager. Leslie—I mean, Ms. Knotts—is trying to reorganize everything and dispose of the old junk."

The two men exchanged glances. Uptight Man B sniffed. Neither of their expressions changed.

"There's years of old files around here. Decades, even," Mark added.

The front door buzzed again, and Mark poked his head into the hall. Leslie juggled her purse, a pizza box, a bag of breadsticks, and two large drinks.

She smiled when she saw him. "Bart, Betty, Yvonne, and Dinah say hi. They were like jackals with fresh meat. I think the whole town is in on the scheme."

Mark hesitated. The Library Ladies were the least of her problems right now. He glanced back into her office. The consultants stood and inched closer to the doorway.

"I'll bring these down to the break room. Come in whenever you're ready."

"Leslie." He stepped into the hallway before she could pass by. Uptight Man A peered through the doorway, both hands clenching his briefcase with a death grip. "These men are from Van Haitsma Consulting."

Leslie's eyes widened, and she tried to shift the boxes and bags balanced in her arms to shake their hands. Mark caught a soda before it tipped.

"Let me take those."

"Thanks," she said to him, then turned to the men. "I'm Leslie Knotts, the new manager of the Carterville branch."

"I am Mr. Black, and this is my associate, Mr. Brown.

As he mentioned, we are from Van Haitsma Consulting. We are here to evaluate this branch."

Mark watched Leslie gather her wits. Her professional façade slipped for a millisecond. A curse flashed through her eyes, but then the calm, cool exterior slipped back into place.

"What can I do for you? Have you eaten lunch?" she asked, gesturing to the pizza boxes in Mark's hands.

Mark's stomach growled. He hoped she wasn't asking them to share. He could eat a whole Bart's Special himself. He was impressed, however, with how professional she sounded. Most people would have been flustered to meet these two without warning or preparation, especially knowing what the consultants could do to their career. They certainly had him wanting to review his last seven tax returns. Leslie, however, sounded as if she'd been preparing for their meeting for a month and had expected them to arrive this afternoon.

Mr. Brown—or was it Mr. Black?—pushed his glasses onto the bridge of his nose again. "No, we haven't."

"Why don't you come with me, and we can have lunch?"

Leslie motioned for the men to proceed down the hallway. Mark followed her, hoping the mousetraps he'd set that morning hadn't sprung.

He placed the boxes on the table and glanced toward the corner. Thankfully, both traps were empty, the smear of peanut butter on the triggers undisturbed. He went to the cupboard for more plates, cups, and napkins and gently nudged the traps to the side of the refrigerator where they'd be out of view.

The two men sat reluctantly at the little table. Mark wouldn't have been surprised if they held their brief-cases in their laps, but they set them down on the right side of their chairs in unison.

Leslie shook the breadsticks out onto an extra plate. "So, what brings you gentlemen to our branch today?"

Uptight Man A pushed his glasses on his nose again and responded, "Our firm has been commissioned by Hanston and Boyd to do a study of the company and rec-ommend growth strategies and areas in which services and assets can be streamlined to meet the rising demands of fluctuating markets." He slid a piece of pizza onto his plate and tried to cut it with his plastic fork.

"Is this study being done company wide?" Leslie asked, handing Mark a plate laden with pizza, bread-sticks, and a cup of ranch dip.

"Would you like me to stay?" he whispered.

"Thanks, but I'll be fine. Enjoy your lunch." She smiled and turned back to the consultants.

Mark took his plate and headed down the hall to the reception area. He pulled a chair out of the debris pile. He wedged a piece of wood under the wobbly leg and sat down to eat his pizza, realizing how much he'd been looking forward to lunch with Leslie. Sitting on this bro-ken chair, he felt like the outcast child in the cafeteria.

He could hear scraps of conversation from down the hall but was glad he didn't have to participate in it. He couldn't make heads or tales out of what the consultants said, but he thought it sounded like bull. If he listened to it all through lunch, he'd fall asleep in his pizza.

He munched on a breadstick. Leslie was answering

questions. She responded promptly and confidently to each thing they asked. The words he could pick out sounded like business jargon, which Mark hated. Why did they have to invent new words for the same old things, just to sound smarter? Like when Uptight Man A said his spiel, why couldn't he say, "We are trying to recommend whom to can?"

Leslie didn't speak like that when she described what she was doing for the company. She kept it straight, and he picked up a lot of tips for his own business. He hoped he'd have time to sit down and get all his paperwork organized in the next couple of weeks. He spent so much time here and at the Lilac Bower, he hadn't done any work on his own house since Christmas. There wasn't any hurry. No one saw the place.

Lunches with Leslie normally stretched into an hour, but now his food was gone in fifteen minutes, and he had no desire to sit on this wobbly chair, staring at the carpet he needed to rip out for another forty-five minutes. He had planned to ask her about the figure-eight race. Leslie put in such long hours. She needed a break. Figuring he might have a chance when the consultants left, Mark rolled his plate into a ball and tossed it into the garbage pile. The plate bounced down the pile, and he heard a snap and a high-pitched scream.

The mousetraps. He hurried to the break room to find Leslie clutching the sides of the table so tightly, her knuckles turned white. Her feet were wrapped around the legs of her chair, and her gaze was locked on the corner where a trap had flipped over, hiding the entire body of the mouse except for the twitching tail.

Mr. Black and Mr. Brown both hoisted their briefcases to their laps and clutched the handles as if the dead mouse would splatter the bubonic plague on the pristine leather.

"I'll take care of this," Mark said, searching through the cupboards for a plastic bag.

"Perhaps a tour of the building and a discussion of the renovations would be in order," Uptight Man B said.

"Definitely." Leslie slowly untangled her feet from the legs of her chair and stood. "We'll start with the reception area."

The two men followed her out in alphabetical order, Uptight Man B glancing over his shoulder to see Mark wrap the bag around his hand and pick up the trap, mouse and all, and reverse the bag. The consultant grimaced and turned his attention back to Leslie. Mark tied the ends and carried it out to the Dumpster.

Men who couldn't handle a dead mouse weren't really men, Mark thought.

Mark spent the rest of the afternoon tearing carpet out of the reception area. Stabbing his utility knife into the carpet and hearing the fibers rip helped his frustration a little. Why he was frustrated, he wasn't going to contemplate. It couldn't be because he'd missed out on an hour of conversation with Leslie. Nor could it be that he was anxious about the consultants for her. He knew the ripping, tearing, and throwing was just what his aggravation needed.

Leslie and the two men had been sequestered in her office all afternoon. He couldn't believe there was that much to talk about. It was almost five o'clock when he cut into the last few feet of carpet. He glanced at her door as she stepped out with the consultants behind her.

One of the consultants made a disparaging comment about the clientele in the area as Mark yanked a particularly big piece of carpet loose, unbalancing himself and knocking him onto his behind. He barely stifled an expletive when he landed on a broken piece of paneling.

If these two men were what all the business people in Chicago were like, Mark couldn't understand why Leslie was so eager to get back. She was definitely out of her element here, but she didn't disparage the locals because they worked blue-collar jobs.

Mr. Brown and Mr. Black glanced at him, but their expressions were as unchanging as those of wax figures. Mark wondered if they'd melt next to an open flame. The consultants said something, and then they all returned to Leslie's office and shut the door again.

Mark threw the last piece of carpet onto the pile, cleaned up his tools, and swept the dust and loose carpet backing pieces into the pile. The consultants still hadn't left.

Mark grabbed his jacket out of the break room and stalked out to his truck. Served him right for waiting until the last minute to ask Leslie about the race.

Chapter Eight

Leslie had stopped breathing when she saw the consultants peeking out of her office behind Mark. They were early; the renovations weren't ready for them. She had expected a couple more weeks, at least. Her project was doomed.

First impressions were key, and hers hadn't been remotely good. She had wanted to present everything at its best, including herself. But her clothes were streaked with dust and her French twist no longer neat. Her armor of clothing and appearance let her down, shaking her confidence.

Despite that, she had tried to remain professional throughout the afternoon. She answered their questions, but her figures were dismal at best. This branch had been average to poor for several years. Mr. Black and Mr. Brown jotted notes on legal pads encased in gleaming leather portfolios on their laps. They even wiped the dust off their chairs with handkerchiefs before sitting. She emphasized the changes she planned for the upcoming tax season—the family-friendly environment for convenience and the new technology for faster service—and how those changes would make this branch a productive asset.

By the end of their visit, Mr. Black and Mr. Brown still looked unimpressed and doubtful.

She handed them their coats, asking when their reports would be completed.

Mr. Black pushed his glasses onto the bridge of his nose. "There are many stages to our data collection and analyzing process. We are still in the initial stages of compiling the necessary data and won't be able to offer any firm recommendations until the latter stages of this process."

"Can you offer any inclination as to what your recommendations might be?" she asked. She knew the question was desperate, but she needed to know something one way or the other.

"We won't be able to reach any definitive conclusions until the preliminary reports have been compiled, and we have a nondisclosure agreement with the partners of Hanston and Boyd. We will not share any recommendation with any staff before it has been written in our report for the partners."

It was well into the evening by the time they left. Leslie was surprised they didn't wipe their shoes on the mat outside the office door.

Leslie felt as if a giant vacuum had sucked out every ounce of her energy. She locked the door and drove home, looking forward to a quiet night, a hot bath, and maybe a Hallmark movie. Anything to keep from agonizing over this dreadful interview and allow her to sleep.

Leslie parked her Honda in the driveway of the Lilac Bower and beeped the doors locked when Minnie barreled out the front door and down the porch steps.

"We're going to be late!" Minnie squawked.

"For what?" Leslie asked, hitching her purse back onto her shoulder.

"It's Ladies' Night Out." Minnie waved to the Buick. "Hurry up! Get in!

"Minnie, I'm not up for it tonight. I've had a long day." She didn't even want to lift her briefcase. She couldn't bear the questioning tonight.

"Oh, honey, Mark told me all about it. You need a drink and time to relax. What better place than with us?"

Leslie thought longingly of the Jacuzzi but allowed herself to be pulled over to Minnie's car. She didn't have the will to resist.

"We'll leave you in peace," Minnie promised.

Leslie doubted that but figured excuses wouldn't help, so she climbed into the Buick. When they arrived at the library, Mark's Suburban idled by the doorway. As she climbed out of the car, Mark waved to her.

"How'd the meeting with the consultants go?" he called.

Leslie waited until she was closer before replying. "I've definitely had better, but I'm not sure I've had worse."

"That good, eh?"

Leslie shook her head and sighed. "I don't know what else I could have done. Nothing could persuade them."

"Did they close the branch?"

"Not on the spot. They said they'd get back to me." Leslie bit her lower lip. It was going to eat at her until she heard from them. She'd spend every waking moment— might as well say every moment, since she wouldn't be sleeping—wondering what they were going to say. Her optimism dwindled by the second. These consultants wouldn't find anything good about construction debris and decades of old paperwork. Her plans were opti- mistic, but they would see them as having no base in re- ality.

"What if I take your mind off things?"

"You mean there's something better than the Ladies' Night Out?" Leslie whispered conspiratorially, "I think they'd be insulted."

"I know, so don't tell them." Mark winked at her. "Even with the spiked punch."

"How'd you know?"

"I've been Minnie's designated driver on more than one occasion."

Leslie stifled a giggle. "So what's better than listening to a bunch of old ladies gossip and drinking adult bever- ages?" She arched an eyebrow at him.

"Hop in and find out." He slapped the vinyl seat be- side him and grinned at her. "Come on."

"I shouldn't skip out on Minnie and the other ladies," Leslie said regretfully. He looked as if he had fun writ- ten all over him tonight.

"Minnie won't mind. In fact, she will be ecstatic.

Remember their matchmaking plans?" He put two fingers between his lips and blew out a shrill whistle. "Aunt Minnie, you don't mind if I steal Leslie away tonight, do you?"

"Not at all." Minnie hurried over, waving her hands. "She wouldn't have any fun with us tonight anyway." Minnie leaned close to Mark and in a stage whisper added, "Edith forgot the punch. We're all going home to check our cabinets. It might take a while. You two go on."

"All right." Leslie walked around the Suburban and pulled open the passenger side door. The door groaned and creaked as it swung on its hinges. She tossed her purse onto the seat. "I take it this door doesn't get used much."

He tilted his head toward the wide-open back area crammed with tools, scraps of lumber, and drywall. "That's who I usually ride with."

Leslie laughed. "No wonder the Library Ladies think they need to work on you."

She tried to raise her foot high enough to step into the truck, but her pencil skirt would not allow her to separate her legs enough.

"What's the deal?" she mumbled, inching her skirt up and trying again. It was the kind of day she was having. First the consultants, and now she couldn't even climb into a truck. If she'd taken a bath, she probably would've drowned.

"What?" Mark leaned across the seat.

"I can't get in. My skirt's too tight."

"Hike it up a little."

"I did. I still can't get in." She tried turning, so she could swing her legs to the side.

"Higher." He chuckled.

"I don't want to do a Britney Spears impression," she said. But she didn't see any other way to get into the vehicle without being hoisted in.

"Your coat goes down to your ankles. It's not as if you're going to flash anyone." Mark grinned at her.

Leslie rolled her eyes and sighed. "Okay, but don't look."

Mark made a big show of turning toward his door, while she bunched her skirt up to the top of her thighs and hopped into the seat. She scooted the fabric down as soon as her behind hit the seat. She snapped her seat belt as Mark shifted out of park and pulled out.

"You could take me home. Minnie'll never know the difference," she said while they waited at a stoplight.

"Minnie will stop there to retrieve something to replace the punch. If she finds you there alone, she'll drag you back to the library."

"I can hide. She won't even know I'm there," Leslie insisted. The Jacuzzi called to her.

"My friend gave me these tickets. They're really hard to get. Practically the whole town will be there. If I show up without you, the Ladies will hear about it before the evening is over."

Leslie sighed. The joys of living in a small town. The gossip traveled faster than her cell phone signal. "I give up. Can't we at least stop there so I can change?" Mark was wearing jeans and a polo shirt under his leather jacket. Her business suit would be overdressed for whatever he had in mind.

He accelerated away from the light. "No time. We're already late."

What else could she expect? She'd been behind the eight ball all day. Things wouldn't turn around now.

"What's better than Ladies' Night Out?" she asked, resigning herself. The streets were almost empty. Only two cars were parked outside the coffee shop.

"Have you ever been to a figure-eight race?"

"A what?" Leslie felt good knowing about Indy and NASCAR, but she'd never heard of a figure-eight race.

"Figure-eight race. The track is in the shape of an eight." He drew an eight in the air with his index finger.

Leslie thought about this. "What do they do when the cars are at the cross? Don't the cars crash?"

"If we're lucky." Mark laughed. "That's what makes it fun."

"But isn't it dangerous?" She was giving up her Jacuzzi for this? Now she doubted her own sanity.

"The tracks are small and dirt, so the drivers can't go very fast. They use old cars that barely run."

When they arrived at the fairgrounds, the parking lot was packed with trucks, minivans, and station wagons. Mark bypassed the entrance to the main parking lot and turned into a service drive. He drove around the building to a snow-covered field already lined with cars.

"This must be quite the event," Leslie commented as Mark backed the Suburban into a spot so narrow she wouldn't have tried parking her Civic in it.

Mark climbed out of the truck. "Races usually draw

people from the whole state. This one is for local racers, so it's a smaller event."

"Smaller event?" Leslie echoed as she heaved the truck door open. "This place is packed. We're parking in a field." Looking down, she realized that the truck was higher off the ground than any vehicle she'd been in except an airplane.

"Most of the other racing events draw professional racing teams and fans from all over the country. In the summers, people are camped out here."

"Tourists." Leslie nodded. "I wondered why they came."

"Once you've been here for a summer, you'll see what it's like." Mark walked around the front of the truck. "Are you getting out or not?"

"I'm scared to jump down. I might twist my ankle."

"It's not that bad." Mark snapped the clasps on his leather jacket and then shoved his hands into his pockets.

"You've never been in heels." She stuck a foot out to show him the pumps she'd worn to the office today. Sensible for the office, but not for jumping out of mammoth vehicles and trekking across snowy fields.

Sighing, Leslie slid slowly off the seat, wincing as her feet slipped into the ankle deep snow. She turned and slammed the door shut. Mark stopped and glanced at her feet. "Follow in my footsteps." He shuffled through the snow, creating a clear path for her to walk in. She stepped into his tracks, lifting her feet daintily out of the snow. Her foot slipped on an icy spot, and she grabbed for Mark's solid body, catching his sleeve. He wrapped an arm around her and pulled her back to her feet.

"My friend Bryce likes to work on cars. I bought the Suburban from him. He has a car in the race, so we've got good seats." He released his hold on her to retrieve the tickets from his pocket.

"Is he driving it?" Leslie asked, feeling strangely fragile without the warmth of Mark's body close to hers.

"Yeah. He's a local legend. He's won the trophy six consecutive years," he said.

"With an increasing family, you'd think he'd want a bigger vehicle," Leslie said as they entered the arena through a smaller door away from the main entrance and the huge crowd of people.

"Judi made him sell it. They bought a minivan." Mark grimaced. "Never want to be saddled with one of those."

Leslie nudged his shoulder. "I thought you weren't a car guy."

"It's not a car thing." Mark handed their tickets to the attendant and led Leslie through the concourse to a stairway that climbed up the arena of seats. "It's a man thing."

Vendors selling carnival snacks wandered the stairs, calling out their wares. Mark grabbed a program thrust at them by a passing worker.

"How so?" Leslie asked, dodging a little boy with a catsup-dripping hot dog.

"There's Judi." Mark waved and started climbing the concrete steps. "The only people who drive minivans are soccer moms and office-supply salesmen. Not me."

Leslie narrowly missed wearing a cone of cotton candy as they passed a group of kids on their way up. "I thought Suburbans were the vehicle of choice for soccer moms."

Mark turned with one foot on the next step. "Not that one."

"Why?" Leslie shouted over the roar of the crowd.

"It has a reputation."

Just then a cheer erupted from the crowd as three off-road go-carts spun around the track. The first had an American flag waving from a long pole. Dirt covered the floor of the arena. Two tractor tires were placed where the holes would be to form the 8-shaped track. The walls of the arena were lined with bales of hay.

"What was that?" Leslie shouted above the cheering.

Mark studied her and then said, "Nothing. They're about to start." He motioned for her to go ahead of him down an aisle of seats.

A woman with a light brown ponytail and an orange sweatshirt with the number twenty-seven emblazoned on it waved to them. "Hey, Mark! Glad you made it."

"Leslie, this is Judi."

Leslie and Judi shook hands.

"Nice to meet you. I saw pictures of your wedding the other night. It looked like a beautiful evening."

"Thank you. I can't believe the Library Ladies roped you into going to a meeting. You're a trouper for staying in town afterward." Judi laughed.

"They were very nice to me," Leslie said, tugging her trench coat off and draping it over the back of her seat.

"Don't get me wrong; they would bend over backward to help a stranger in need. But they are always looking for fresh meat for their schemes. Don't let them suck you in."

"They already tried. I thought I'd warded them off

until Minnie sent Mark up to my room with dinner after I told her I was taking a shower."

"They are getting more creative. I have to give them that." Judi shook her head.

The first notes of "The Star-Spangled Banner" played, and the crowd rose to its feet. The song finished, and the announcer listed the first heat of drivers.

"I can't believe there are so many people here." Leslie craned her neck to see around the arena. "Is the whole town here?"

"Most of it. A lot of local businesses sponsor cars," said Judi.

"Did you sponsor Bryce's?" she asked Mark.

"Yeah. I spray-painted my name across the trunk."

"Where's the rest of the Bryce cheering squad?" Mark asked, propping one foot on the seat in front of them.

Leslie's gaze focused on the denim stretched across his knee. Her fingers itched to smooth a fold in the fabric. She folded her hands in her lap to keep them from acting of their own volition. What was wrong with her? Exhaustion. It must be. It made her easily distracted by muscular objects. Well, one in particular. Mark. She clenched her hands tighter and directed her attention to what Judi said about Bryce's friends.

"Dan is towing. Noah is with the fire crew, and the rest are playing pit crew," Judi replied.

"Towing?" Leslie asked, looking at Mark.

Mark leaned across Leslie to talk to Judi. "I had to explain what a figure-eight race was." He winked at Leslie.

"I still don't get it."

"You'll find out soon enough. They're lining up the

first heat of cars." Judi pointed to the other end of the arena. Cars with the exhaust pipes puffing out of the hoods and beams of steel welded across the doors idled next to a bale of hay with a red flag stuck in the middle. Most were spray-painted with messages acknowledging families, friends, and sponsors.

"Is Bryce in this one?" Mark asked Judi.

"He's in the next heat. He has an orange Pinto with the number twenty-seven painted on the side," Judi said. "It's obnoxiously ugly, but that's what happens when you let a sponsor like Mark choose colors."

Leslie laughed. "He's told me about his mishaps with color. So I'm still trying to figure out this eight thing. They race around those tractor tires?" She pointed to the dirt field.

Judi nodded. "First one to complete ten laps wins."

"How do they keep track of the laps?"

"The officials watch each car and keep track." Judi pointed to the men placed around the arena in orange shirts and black pants carrying two-way radios and flags. "It's usually not hard to tell which car is winning."

Leslie was going to ask why, but the official waved the flag, and the cars took off, filling the arena with the roar of their engines. There were four cars in the heat, and it was a motley mix. A station wagon with the wagon part pushed into the back seat led into the first turn, followed by a midsize sedan painted like *The General Lee,* and a Buick Century. A Plymouth something or other stalled at the starting line, the helmeted driver pounding on the dashboard and rocking in his seat.

Leslie found herself laughing and gasping with the

rest of the crowd as the other cars steered into the tight turns and spun out into the bales of straw around the outside of the arena. Mud flew from their tires, and smoke coughed from the exhausts. The wagon easily distanced itself from the other vehicles and barreled around them on the corners. The entire crowd gasped when the front wheel of the wagon broke loose from its axle and rolled away from the car, immobilizing the wagon in the crosshairs of the eight. The other cars tried to squeeze around it but couldn't. The Buick slammed into the rear of the wagon and steadily pushed it aside, flinging an arc of mud from its tires. As soon as the path was clear, *The General Lee* look-a-like gunned the gas, spun around the final turn, and crossed the finish line.

"That was great!" Leslie exclaimed. Each crash of metal on metal had knocked an ounce of her tension away. "I've never seen anything like it. Are there more races?" She glanced at Mark.

He grinned at her. "There's usually about ten with all the heats and the finals."

The tow trucks came out and pulled the wagon and the Plymouth out of the arena while a front-end loader adjusted the position of the tractor tires. A race official collected the broken front wheel and tossed in onto the hood of the wagon as the tow truck pulled it out of the arena. Soon the next line of cars was ready.

"That's Bryce, in the second row." Judi pointed.

As the cars took off, Judi stood up to cheer. Bryce quickly took the lead, maneuvering around the corners easily. He lapped the other cars and was on his way to victory. Two of the cars crashed into each other, and one dragged its rear bumper as it lumbered around the track. Bryce tried to scoot past it on the curve but drove over the bumper, tearing it loose from the other car and dragging it behind his own.

"His rear tires are flat," Leslie said, as Bryce rounded the last turn. "How can he keep going?"

"Flat tires aren't a problem. If your car moves, you keep driving." Mark laughed. "Sometimes having a soft tire helps."

"He's got more tires in the pit, too. When this race is over, the boys will have the flat ones off in no time, and he'll be ready for the semis," replied Judi between cheers and whistles.

Leslie looked at them both skeptically. Her dad had practically burst a blood vessel when she drove a mile on a flat once.

Bryce limped through the last lap of the race. Judi stood up and hollered, "Go, Bryce! That's my man!"

Leslie stood and clapped, too. She might have let out a whoop of excitement herself. Judi threw her arms around her and jumped up and down when Bryce crossed the finish line. Leslie felt some of her bobby pins come loose during the jostling. When she reached up to repair the damage, a lock of hair came completely loose. She'd need a mirror to fix it.

She leaned over to Judi to ask her where the ladies' room was. Judi gave her directions. Leslie's stomach growled as she turned. "Guess I'm hungry, too. Can I get anyone anything on my way back?"

Mark requested a soda and Judi an elephant ear. Leslie wasn't sure what that was, but after her stupid question about the flat tires, she didn't want to ask. She was sure it'd be obvious when she got to the concession stands. Mark stood to allow her to slide past him. Scooting past him without brushing against the entire length of his body was nearly impossible. She hoped he didn't notice the unsteadiness in her steps from the slight contact.

Chapter Nine

Judi leaned closer to Mark. "I thought you were aware of the Library Ladies' schemes."

"Yeah, so?" Mark said, leaning back in his seat and propping a foot on the back of seat in front of him. He'd forgotten Judi was almost a junior member of the Ladies. She'd have pity on Leslie and leave her alone, but she'd have no compassion for him.

"This is a date, isn't it?" Judi asked, pushing the sleeves of her sweatshirt up. A sure sign she was about to do some digging.

"No." He shook his head. "No way. It's not a date."

"Would you like to protest some more or give in?" Judi laughed, lightly punching him on the shoulder.

"It's not a date," Mark hedged, rolling his program into a tight cylinder. It wasn't a date. He was helping out a friend. An attractive friend, he acknowledged,

103

remembering how her hips swayed as she descended the stairs, but a friend nonetheless.

"You know the Ladies will see exactly what they want to see." Judi propped her feet against the seat back in front of her.

As do you, he didn't say. He had to tell her about the charade. Judi would keep digging if he didn't. He knew she'd be discreet, having been a victim of the schemes herself. "That's what we're hoping. We have an agreement."

"You and Minnie?" Judi asked. "She gonna let you off the hook until you finish the Lilac Bower?"

"No. Me and Leslie."

"And what is this agreement?" Judi turned to face him. Mark pitied Boppy when he was old enough to get into trouble. His mother wasn't going to let any excuse slide.

"We are pretending to date until she leaves. That will keep Minnie and her friends off both our backs."

"Wishful thinking."

"It's worth a try." He sighed. If Judi wouldn't play along, he and Leslie might as well give up the charade.

"I'm not saying it's a bad idea, but I don't think anything will keep the Library Ladies at bay. Unless you plan to engage in public displays of affection." Judi wiggled her eyebrows.

Mark shifted uncomfortably. "They're letting me get some work done. I've had a whole week without any interruptions."

Judi nodded slowly. "You won't be able to keep them from finding out. What if things go wrong with you and Leslie? What if you decide you can't stand each other?"

"Leslie's trying to get a promotion back to the corporate headquarters. She thinks it'll only be a couple more months. I can put up with anything for that long." He moved his foot back to the floor when the occupant of the seat in front of him returned. "Keep this between us, okay? Bryce will be a pain if he finds out."

"You think he won't figure it out? He's as bad as Minnie. He's been asking if I've met any new female teachers recently."

Mark only managed to shut his gaping jaw by pushing it closed with one hand. "Bryce, I can handle. Even if Leslie turns into a witch, it would be better than having the Ladies arranging meetings at every turn. I've got enough work that I can't be running across town to give rides to stranded women every day."

"Business is picking up? What do you have lined up besides the Lilac Bower?"

"I'm remodeling Leslie's office."

Judi raised her eyebrows. "I thought you were answering phones, filing. That sort of thing."

Mark explained the remodeling project. "We've had lunch together most days this week."

"Uh-huh," Judi said with a penetrating look.

Mark scowled back. He reminded himself to never let Judi fill an empty spot on poker night. She'd clean him out. "I thought we already had this conversation."

"But this changes things." Judi studied him.

Mark tried not to flinch under her steady gaze. Judi was his friend, he told himself. Maybe she was trying to help him learn something about himself. No, he decided, she liked to pick on him.

"It changes nothing." Mark scratched the back of his neck.

"Sure. You've got the Suburban." Judi propped her chin on her hand and grinned.

"Whatever." Mark turned to look around the arena. People were still filing in and out of the entrance. He spied Leslie at the bottom of the stairs across the arena. She scanned the seats, looking bewildered. He waved to her when she glanced across the field. He saw her shake her head and turn back up the staircase to the concourse.

"Why'd you bring her here?"

"I told you." He glanced at Judi out of the corner of his eye.

"We both know that's baloney." She patted him on the shoulder.

"She had a rough day."

"Spending the evening with the Library Ladies and their punch sounds like just the thing for a rough day."

"And being harassed about me or any other guy in town is not." *Nor is it what* I *wanted to deal with,* he thought.

"This keeps getting more interesting." Judi shook her head.

"It's nothing," he said more gruffly than he intended.

"Keep telling yourself that. Maybe one of us will believe it."

"Whatever." Maybe if he stopped talking, Judi would leave him alone. She'd made him question his motives for bringing Leslie to the figure-eight race, and he didn't want to reconsider them.

Leslie climbed the stairs with a tray of drinks balanced in one hand and two elephant ears in the other. Mark jumped up in such a hurry, his folding seat sprang back into position with a snap. He spared it a quick glance and hurried down the stairs.

"Whatever," Judi called after him.

When he reached Leslie, he tried to grab an elephant ear because it was going to slip off her plate.

"I don't think so." Leslie handed him the tray of drinks. "I'm not letting that out of my grasp."

"I love elephant ears," Mark said, following her up the stairs. His gaze drifted to her skirt and the way it slipped across her hips as she climbed. He would blame Judi for that, also. He wouldn't have glanced at her skirt if Judi hadn't suggested he felt more than friendship for Leslie.

"Then you should have asked me to get you one." She stopped abruptly and turned. "Because you're not getting one bite of this one." She grinned at him and scooted down the aisle to the seat beside Judi. She tore off a piece of the sugary dough and plopped it into her mouth.

Mark took a deep breath, his eyes fixed on the sugar clinging to her lips. He would blame Judi. It was all her fault. He hadn't been thinking about Leslie in that way at all. Not until Judi brought it up. Not until she made him think this was a date. Leslie was only a friend, and he was trying to be a good one back by cheering her up.

Baloney.

But that was all they would be. Leslie would leave Carterville when she got that promotion she wanted. The consultants had to be impressed with her knowledge and her vision for the future. She'd be heading back to Chicaso in a few months.

They could have a good time now, and that's all it would be. A good time and some relief from the schemes of the Library Ladies.

Leslie laughed at something Judi said. Sugar clung to her lips, and she licked it off slowly. Mark forced himself to close his mouth and take a deep breath.

"People are still coming in. The line at the ticket window is a mile long," Leslie said, pulling off a bite-size piece of elephant ear and handing it to him. "You can have this piece if you don't mind my fingers."

Mark grabbed the piece and popped the sweetness into his mouth.

"When does the next race start?" Leslie asked.

"Any minute. These are the semifinals." Mark glanced at the starting area. Cars ambled up to the starting line. He forced himself to concentrate on the cars and not on Leslie licking sugar off her fingertips.

People filed up the stairs, scanning for open spots. There were enough seats at the end of their row for a family of five. The family filed in with the father cramming himself into the seat next to Mark. Mark angled his legs to one side to give the man more room and brushed against Leslie's leg. He shot a furtive look her way to see if she had noticed. She was facing Judi and waving her hands about something. He let his leg fall against hers, delighted she didn't move away.

During the next race, he realized how much fun Leslie was having. She shifted in her seat and cheered as her favorite car pulled ahead and fell behind. Her every movement radiated through his thigh and up his body. He could barely concentrate on the following race.

"Which car do you think is going to win this one?" Mark asked Leslie as she folded the paper plate from her elephant ear into quarters.

Leslie studied the cars as they chugged up to the starting line.

"The big cars don't seem to do well." She tapped a manicured finger against her lips. "I think the light blue one with the thirty-four painted on the side." The hood was crumpled, and the rear bumper had been replaced with a wooden plank.

"That one?" Mark asked. It's the one he would have picked.

"You have a better pick?"

"I'd put money on the Pontiac," Mark said, after scanning the rest of the cars.

"Which one is that?"

He leaned closer to her and pointed. "Second row on the right."

"You'd bet on that one, huh?"

"Yeah." Mark shrugged and faced Leslie. Her eyes glittered in merriment.

"How much?"

Mark hesitated. "Five bucks."

Leslie held out her hand. "I'll take that bet."

They shook hands as the cars took off. Leslie's car jumped ahead early, while Mark's car limped around the second turn and grumbled to a stop.

"Looks like I win." Leslie tugged the sleeve of Mark's sweatshirt.

"The race isn't over yet." He gestured to the track where the rest of the cars still spun around in the mud.

"But your car is dead." She waved her hand at the track. The driver of the stalled car jumped out and stood behind the cement barriers. "The driver's even given up on it."

"Your car hasn't won." He pointed to the track where a rusted Cadillac bumped Leslie's car to the side.

"It beat yours," she said indignantly.

"That wasn't the bet."

Leslie's eyes narrowed, and Mark couldn't help but grin back.

"We bet on which car would win the race, not which car would beat the other," he reminded her.

"You're just trying to get out of paying me five bucks."

"I am not. It's what we bet," Mark insisted.

Leslie's car passed the Cadillac and pushed it into the barriers around the final turn, finally winning the race.

"There. Now. I've won. Five bucks, right here." She held her palm out to Mark, flashing a dazzling smile at him.

Mark sighed and dug into his rear pocket. He pulled out a well-worn wallet and slid out a five-dollar bill. He brushed it across Leslie's palm.

"Double or nothing?" He grinned.

"How deep is that wallet?" Leslie grabbed the hand with the wallet and pulled it toward her. Her fingertips were cool, but her touch burned his skin. He was momentarily speechless at the contrast of her smooth skin and polished nails against his calloused hand. "Hmm. That's looking kinda thin. I think I'll take the five dollars." She let go of his wrist and slipped the bill from his other hand. She folded the bill in half. Then she stopped and held it up between her fingers. "Let's make the stakes more interesting."

"Like what?"

Leslie pursed her lips. "How about a neck massage?"

"A what?" Mark's stomach grew hot.

"My neck and shoulders get really sore."

"You want me to give you a neck massage?" Mark's throat was dry, and his heart pounded. His thoughts should not be going in this direction. He had to stop thinking this way. It was pointless. Leslie wanted this charade, and he had to respect that. This was supposed to be fake for him, too.

"You don't have to do it. You could hire someone." Leslie rolled her head from side to side. "I had a great masseuse in Chicago. I went once a week. It was wonderful. But expensive. Are you expecting to lose again?"

"No . . . I . . . No." Mark covered his mouth with one hand. "Match race or pick the winner?"

"Match race? What's that?"

"We pick two cars, and whoever's car finishes before the other wins."

"Match race, then. I don't want any discrepancies over the winner." Leslie slapped her hands on her thighs. "This is fantastic."

"I've had this awful kink right back here." Mark lifted his shoulder and traced a muscle along his shoulder blade.

Leslie glanced at him and went back to surveying the cars as they lined up. "Since I feel so sorry for you, I'll let you pick a car first."

Mark studied the cars. He pointed to a Ford LTD

painted like a cow, complete with floppy ears and a mud-caked tail. "The cow car."

"Really?" Leslie gave him a horrified look.

He nodded, knowing he had a dumb grin on his face. It didn't matter whether he picked a good car or not. This was a win-win situation for him. Either he had his hands on her or she had hers on him, and that prospect sounded better by the moment.

She scooted to the edge of her seat and scanned the field. "I want the car with the NAPA hat on the top."

"Start flexing your fingers."

"Don't hold your breath." Leslie slapped his knee.

Mark's leg muscles tightened in response. He willed them to relax. He was beginning to think his agreement with Leslie was the equivalent of playing with matches at a gas station. You never knew when it would explode.

The cars took off. The cow car and the NAPA car flew around the first corner, rubbing fenders the whole way.

The cars were neck and neck throughout the race. On the final turn, Leslie's car pushed Mark's car to the outside of the turn and into the cement barriers. Her car crossed the finish line and stalled.

"I won!" she screamed, jumping from her seat. She grinned at Mark when she sat back down.

"Double or nothing?" He grinned back. Someone needed to slap him and shake him out of this, because he obviously wasn't keeping himself out of trouble.

"I wouldn't want you to get into unmanageable back-rub debt. Gambling is addictive."

"Bryce's car is in the next race. I've got a sure thing."

"I wouldn't bet against him. You said he won the last

six times. You can work on getting your fingers flexible for my neck rub." She turned away from him to say something to Judi.

Bryce made it into the finals, whipping his orange Pinto around the curves and weaving between the other cars. By the last race, everyone in the stands was on their feet.

Mark had been painfully aware of every movement Leslie made and was glad the event was almost over.

He hadn't been this attracted to anyone in a long time. Why was Leslie different?

He didn't want to and didn't need to think about that. Leslie would be leaving as soon as she turned the office around. They could be friends and enjoy the benefits of the charade.

Friends?

What had he been thinking, agreeing to bet a neck massage?

He forced himself to concentrate on the race. He echoed Judi's and Leslie's cheers as Bryce squeaked ahead of a Monte Carlo to take the checkered flag.

Judi jumped up and down and whistled through her fingers. She pushed past them to run down the stairs. Mark grabbed Leslie's hand and guided her through the throngs of people to the pit area where Bryce and his pit crew celebrated.

Chapter Ten

Five men stood around the mud-covered Pinto. Judi leaped into the arms of the dirtiest man, who Leslie guessed was Bryce. He was covered with mud except for a goggle-shaped area around his eyes. Despite the layer of dirt, Bryce had rugged good looks and a charismatic smile.

Mark gave Bryce a high five and introduced Leslie.

"Congratulations," Leslie said. She hung back as the guys looked over the car and talked about the various things they had adjusted to make it better. Mark nodded and asked general questions, but Leslie could see he wasn't all that interested in the mechanics.

"My eyes glaze over when they start talking cars," Judi said, joining Leslie by the trailer.

"Me, too" Leslie said. "All I know about cars is where to put the gas."

"I almost agreed to having my blinker fluid changed once," Judi said. "Bryce takes care of the car now."

114

They watched the guys point to something under the fender and then making a wrenching motion.

"Have these guys been friends for a long time?" Leslie asked.

"Most of them have been together since high school, like Mark and Bryce."

"How long have you known Bryce?"

"We met shortly after I started teaching here." Judi laughed when Leslie's jaw dropped open. "You were expecting a story involving the Library Ladies."

"Well, yeah." Leslie shrugged. "They told me they were involved, but that you and Bryce knew nothing about it."

"Everyone knows when the Ladies are involved. They made a lucky guess is how it happened."

"What happened?" Bryce said, diverting his attention from the discussion of tire treads.

"I was telling Leslie about how we started dating. She's been to the Ladies' Night Out."

"A bunch of nosy busybodies." Bryce rolled his eyes and shook his head.

"Be nice," Judi chided him. "Your mother's in the group."

"She's the worst one." He stood up, wiping his hands on his jeans. "Leslie, watch yourself. They've been stuck on Mark for a while now." He slapped Mark on the shoulder and shook his head. "I'd give up if I were them. Who'd want this?"

"All this fame and glory goes to his head." Judi gestured to the trophy resting on the hood of the car. "He's only this obnoxious during a race. Normally, he's a pretty nice guy."

"I'm lucky she puts up with me," Bryce said, kissing Judi on the cheek.

"I'm the only one who stuck it out for more than two dates, dear," Judi said, wiping the smudge of dust off her face.

Bryce wandered back to the car. Judi turned to Leslie and whispered, "I know about your charade. Mark told me."

Leslie's chest tightened. If he told everyone, how would they keep the scheme from the Library Ladies? She bit her lower lip.

Judi reached over and squeezed her shoulder. "It's okay. I beat it out of him. I won't tell anyone."

Leslie sighed in relief. "Have the Ladies really tried to set him up six times?"

"Mark makes it sound worse than it actually is, but they've been focused on him since last summer. They can't seem to get him to take the bait."

"The ones he told me about were beyond ridiculous. The car thing, especially. How can they think he won't figure it out?"

"Yeah, the Ladies need to work on their subtlety. If he smells a trap, he's turned off. He'll be polite about it, but when the scheme is done, he is, too."

Mark wiped his hands on his jeans as he stood up. "Leslie, they've invited us to go out for drinks," he said. "Would you like to go? I know you've had a long day, and if you don't want to go . . ."

Judi gave him a funny look. He stared back at her. "What?"

"Nothing," Judi said, a smile tugging at her lips.

"Anyway." He moved to block Judi from the conversation. "Would you like to go?"

"Sure," Leslie agreed happily. She was having a good time. She didn't look forward to going back to her room to stew about what the consultants thought and agonize over the reports she needed to gather. Mark had been right. This was exactly what she needed.

She followed Mark back to the Suburban and discreetly hitched up her skirt to haul herself into the vehicle. Her thoughts kept wandering back to what Judi had said about Mark's not liking things shoved in his face. She glanced at him as he drove around the parking lot to where Bryce and the rest of the gang were parked. He was a grown man. She didn't blame him for wanting to make his own decisions.

They formed a train of vehicles and ended up at a crowded bar. Judi and Bryce led the way inside. Bryce had his arm around Judi, and they walked almost in step, their bodies moving against each other as smoothly as a well-oiled machine. Bryce leaned down and kissed Judi's temple.

Suddenly, Leslie felt very lonely. She pulled the lapels of her trench coat tighter around her neck, blocking out the cold air creeping through the silk of her blouse. She shoved her hands into her pockets so she wouldn't be tempted to reach for Mark's arm.

They entered the bar, and a cheer rose up from the diners. Leslie stepped backward, bumping into Mark. He put a hand on her arm to steady her.

Bryce raised a fist into the air and let out a Rebel yell, and Leslie jumped.

"Seven years in a row!" he yelled.

The crowd cheered again.

Judi and Bryce led them to a large circular booth in a corner. On their way, several of the guests reached out to slap hands with Bryce. He must know everyone in the room, Leslie thought. Had she entered Carterville's version of *Cheers*?

Leslie took a seat next to Judi, relieved to be out of the spotlight Bryce generated, and Mark sat on her other side. Memorabilia from the local high school decorated the walls. Televisions perched in corners at either end of the room with various sporting events muted. On the shelf above their booth were six trophies like Bryce's. Next to each was a framed photograph of a grinning Bryce.

The waitress came for their drink orders. Leslie requested the same wine cooler Judi ordered.

Throughout the rest of the evening, she chatted with Judi, surprised at how easily they conversed. It was as if they had been friends since they were children, even though they had very few shared experiences. Judi had taught second grade until Boppy was born and then stayed home to take care of him. She'd looked forward to being a mother most of her life.

Leslie had never considered whether she actually wanted children or if she even liked them. Children weren't in her life plan. She focused entirely on her career and hadn't thought about a family or home. Her school counselors had helped her scope out her climb up the corporate ladder. She had planned on four years to get her CPA and making partner by age thirty. She had been well on her way until Chuck derailed her.

The scowl formed on her face before she could stop it. She reached for her drink and took a long sip. She would overcome that obstacle and show the consultants she was worth more than a branch manager of a barely existent branch. She stiffened her spine as well as her resolve. Chuck Silverman wasn't going to affect her career anymore.

Chuck, the consultants, the branch, and the miserable state of her career. She hadn't thought about any of it all evening. She shook her head a little. She'd obsessed about it every minute since Chuck told her the consultants were coming. It should be wrenching her stomach now that they had visited and it had gone less than well. Less than well? It had been a disaster. They'd written her off as soon as they saw the pile of trash in the middle of the office, if not before.

She should be scheming, arranging, planning for something to improve their evaluation, but instead she sipped wine coolers with a group of people who had a relationship to dust and car exhaust she'd never known existed, and she enjoyed it.

Maybe it was the alcohol or maybe it was the people, but this was the first time she'd had fun in a long time. She had gone out with people from work for drinks, but it had never been this relaxing. Mark and Bryce poked fun at each other and slapped each other on the back. Whenever she went out with people from work, she felt as if she should watch what she said and how she behaved or one of them would use it against her. The laughter hadn't hurt her stomach or brought tears to her eyes; it had been strained and polite, the way you laughed when the smelly guy on the subway told you a knock-knock joke.

Perhaps spending a few months or even a year stuck in Carterville wouldn't be as horrible as she'd thought when she was banished there.

She was disappointed when Bryce and Judi stood to leave, claiming the need to rescue Grandma from Boppy or vice versa. Leslie wanted to hold the evening forever. Even the meeting this afternoon didn't seem so bad when these people surrounded her.

Bryce laughed as Leslie tried to hoist herself into the Suburban. She turned around and gave him a dirty look. She wasn't hitching up her skirt in front of a crowd.

"I can't get into this thing." She gave Judi a pleading look. "How'd you do it?"

"I rarely wore skirts, for one thing!" Judi laughed. "Mark will kill me, but he knows exactly how I got into the truck." She tilted her head toward Mark.

Mark slammed his door shut and walked around the truck. "Judi. If a word of this leaks to your mother. Or Aunt Minnie, so help me . . ."

Leslie squealed when Mark placed his hands on her hips. He lifted her easily up into the seat. Leslie had never felt the air rush out of her lungs so quickly. She clutched the edge of the seat, willing her heartbeat to stop throbbing in her ears. He might as well have put her into a hot-air balloon, with the unsteadiness she felt.

"Bryce had to give up the truck when he couldn't lift me anymore. I was nine months pregnant and weighed slightly less than a baby elephant."

"You walked like one, too," Bryce said, scratching his chin.

Judi gave him a playful swat on the behind. "You'd better watch it, mister." Judi gave Bryce a playful stern look.

"I love you, honey." He kissed Judi on the cheek and waved to Mark and Leslie. "Glad you got to see me."

Mark shut Leslie's door and returned to his side of the vehicle. He climbed in and jammed the key into the ignition.

Leslie fumbled for her seat belt and clicked it. "I thought you said Judi made him sell this because she wanted a minivan. She made it sound as if Bryce wanted to sell it."

"She made Bryce think he wanted to sell it." He cranked the engine over.

"How's that?"

"It's what women do. They get into a guy's head, and suddenly he's doing things he would never do." He maneuvered the Suburban out of the parking lot.

"Like selling this truck?"

"Bryce loved this thing. It was his baby. Everybody knew it."

"Probably because he had to manhandle his dates to take them anywhere." Leslie laughed.

"Not that any of them minded." Mark shook his head.

"Are you sure?"

"Bryce was the man." Mark tapped the steering wheel with his palm.

"Bryce was the town playboy, and the Suburban was his mansion? Poor Judi. How did she put up with it?"

"Poor Judi, my ass. Girls fought each other to go out

with him. He didn't have to ask anyone to the senior prom because two girls duked it out over him."

"Literally? They did not." When Mark nodded, she asked, "How'd the loser take it?"

"She got me as the consolation prize." Mark turned away.

"That's nothing to turn your nose up at." Leslie bit her lip. "I bet the girls lined up for you as well."

Mark snorted. "Were the girls in your school lining up to date the president of the theatre club?"

"The president of our theatre club was a girl."

"You know what I mean."

"No, they weren't. But that doesn't mean you were a dork. You could have dated whomever you wanted. You only had to ask them out."

"I did ask a few, but they used me as a stepping stone to Bryce. They always wanted to double with him and his flavor of the week. Girls even asked me out. You know, get in with the cool guy's dorky best friend, and maybe you'll catch the cool guy's attention. Sometimes it worked. Sometimes it didn't. Bryce dated enough of them to keep them trying."

"He dated that much?"

"Yeah. He had a new girl every week or two. He wasn't much for commitment. He wanted to have fun. Until Judi came along. Then he bought a minivan."

Leslie gave him a bewildered look. "And you ended up with the truck?"

"It hasn't lured any Pamela Anderson wannabe's my way, but it's great for work. I can haul all my tools and even a lot of materials."

"I'm not sure I want to be seen in this vehicle now. The symbol of Bryce's swinging bachelorhood," Leslie said, looking out the window at the darkened houses. "People might get the wrong impression of me."

Mark turned the Suburban onto the main road.

"Or maybe I do. Try out the alter ego thing," she said, staring out the window. "Nobody around here knows the real me. I could try something different. See if I would enjoy a life that is different than my plan."

"You aren't going to start wearing tights and a cape?" Mark gave her a half grin.

"I said *alter ego,* not *super hero,*" she said, laughing. "I can try something besides the anal-retentive workaholic I normally am. You know, less Lois Lane, more Lana Lang."

It might feel good to shed her corporate exterior for a while. She rarely had the opportunity to wear anything besides business suits in the city. Things were different here. She could try some more casual clothes, maybe even some jeans.

"Lana Lang?"

"She was a cheerleader or something. From *Superman*. Clark Kent's girlfriend in high school."

Mark parked the Suburban in Minnie's driveway. "I know who she is."

He walked around and opened the door as Leslie unbuckled her seat belt and scooted to the edge of the opening. She tried to prepare herself for the electricity of his hands as they grasped her waist, but the sparks shot through her more swiftly than before. He set her carefully on the ground but didn't let go. She slowly lifted her eyes to his face.

The streetlight glowed on one side of his face while casting the other in shadow. He stared intently at Leslie, his gaze traveling over her face.

Leslie could feel her chest rising and falling as if she had climbed into the Suburban rather than been lifted out. She let her gaze rise from the collar of his polo shirt up to his face.

When their eyes met, he whispered, "*Superman* is my favorite movie."

He bent forward and lightly touched his lips to hers. The smell of sawdust and soap overtook her. His lips moved across hers gently, encouraging her, asking her if she wanted more.

He tightened his grip on her waist and pulled her closer to him. Her eyes fluttered closed. She felt his life, his strength, encompassing her as he deepened the kiss.

She allowed it. No, that wasn't true. She embraced it, gloried in it, relishing the freedom and the heat. She inched her hands up his chest, testing the muscle definition evident through the cotton fabric. After a few moments, he eased his hold on her and released her mouth. He pushed a stray strand of hair behind her ear.

"I had a good time tonight, Leslie," he said, his voice ragged.

He took her hand and walked her to the door of the Lilac Bower.

"Good night," she whispered. "I had a good time, too. It was just what I needed."

Chapter Eleven

Leslie went into the office early on Monday morning. She wanted to get there before Mark showed up. She told herself she wanted to start on the paperwork before Mark started banging around. She told herself she wasn't trying to avoid Mark, but she knew that wasn't true. She'd spent the whole weekend avoiding both Minnie and Mark.

When Leslie had climbed the stairs after kissing Mark, she had noticed Minnie's light blink off. Minnie's room faced the driveway, and her window had the perfect view of the Suburban. That had been confirmed when Minnie waved to her from the window when Leslie left to go shopping Saturday morning.

Leslie plunked her purse onto the now empty chair across from her desk and tossed her keys on top of it. She had reduced the piles of folders and papers to a few stacks on the floor and now had chairs available. She settled herself at her desk and started to organize the papers she would need to complete the reports.

She could have kicked herself for forgetting about her agreement with Mark. She had forgotten they would have to put on a show occasionally. Mark had obviously noticed Minnie's light and decided to prick his aunt's curiosity. Leslie hadn't noticed it before they kissed, and she let herself get carried away. But when she floated up the stairs to her room and passed by Minnie's door, she saw the light shining out from under it. Mark probably thought she was desperate. Or trying to be more like one of Bryce's dates in her new alter ego.

She should have called him right away Saturday morning and apologized for overdoing it, but she wasn't ready to talk to him. She didn't want to know what he thought. She didn't want to admit to herself it had all been fake—at least on his part. Or that she had forgotten their agreement so quickly.

Normally, she didn't hide from problems or confrontations. She faced them and resolved them. But now she needed some time. She'd never faced this problem before.

She decided to spend Saturday shopping at the mall in the next town. She needed retail therapy.

The mall had a wider variety of stores than Leslie had expected. Several stores carried well-tailored business suits, but she looked at them without her normal enthusiasm. She walked out of each of the stores empty-handed. She didn't need anything. She fingered the brightly colored silk scarves, debating whether she needed another one she would never wear.

She wandered into a casual clothing store, drawn to the wall of denim at the rear. She had a pair or two of jeans she never wore with the rest of her stuff in storage. She was feeling a little daring. Maybe she could buy another pair.

She felt as if she needed something different. Something outside of herself. Something that wasn't already hanging in her closet in another color.

Denim would also be practical when she got to the papers in the basement. She already had two suits that couldn't be reclaimed from the dust even by a good dry cleaner.

Most of the clothes she'd brought to Carterville were too dressy for the events she had been to. Not that she was a social butterfly; she'd only been to the library and a figure-eight race. While that was plural, it hardly counted as a bustling social calendar. Anyway, no one at the figure-eight race was wearing linen pants or business suits.

With trepidation she studied the jeans hanging on the wall. Her desire for something different faded as the fears of stepping out of her safe, protective suits grew. Finally she grabbed several pairs and rushed into the fitting room. Trying them on hadn't helped. She didn't look like herself in any of them. But that was the point, she reminded herself. She had to buy at least one pair.

After wavering for half an hour between pairs, she finally went with the salesgirl's advice and bought them both. She also purchased a couple of T-shirts and a navy V-neck sweater.

Buying a more casual wardrobe did not mean she wanted to be here for a long time. She was still going to fight for her promotion. Which meant, she reminded herself, hunkering down and tackling the reports.

She clicked the power on her laptop and started entering figures. She was so engrossed in charts and forecasts, she sprang out of her seat when the phone rang. She tapped SAVE and then answered the phone, only to hear Chuck laughing on the other end.

"How'd the afternoon with the consultants go?"

"Did you know they were coming? You could have warned me." She tapped the end of her pen on a stack of paper.

"If I did that, it would be like we were friends," he mused aloud into the phone. Leslie pictured him leaning back at his desk with his feet propped on the edge. She knew a little push would flip his chair, and she smiled.

"We are friends. You warned me they were coming to begin with. That's what friends do." Never mind that he had an ulterior motive of protecting his own behind, it had still helped her. She rubbed her forehead. The first twinges of a migraine flickered behind her eyes. It was the sound of his voice, like Pee-wee Herman on helium. "Do you have a point?"

"I was wondering how it went."

"You're hoping I crashed and burned, and you want to gawk at the traffic accident."

"I knew you blew it." Chuck laughed into the phone. "How badly did you crack under the pressure?"

Leslie rolled her eyes, hoping Chuck would tip back too far in his chair and smack his head. Not that putting a dent in the back of his skull would incapacitate Chuck noticeably.

"What do you want, Chuck?"

"Oh, yes."

She heard papers shuffling. He was deliberately stalling.

"It has to do with your construction project. How is that progressing, by the way? Close to being finished?"

"The ugly is gone, but it's not done yet. What about it?"

"Wintley pulled their account out," he said gleefully. "So we're cutting your construction budget."

"What does that matter? They aren't connected with this branch at all." Wintley was a prestigious account but not a major source of funding. She'd never even worked on the account.

"Pendworth, Maltoy, and Stoddard followed."

"Oh." Those were the three biggest accounts at Hanston and Boyd. This would throw headquarters into a tailspin. Leslie stared at the troll snow-globes on her desk. She needed to get rid of those. Their hair reminded her of Chuck's. "Where'd they go?"

"Hanston and Boyd split. Mr. Hanston took those four clients with him."

"And about half the revenue. Wow." She grabbed a snow-globe and shook it, sending iridescent sparkles swirling around the troll's hair.

"I guess Ms. Boyd knew it was coming; that's why she hired the consultants. Mr. Hanston found out about them and pulled out immediately. Ms. Boyd is scrambling. She's cutting budgets and special projects left and right. I can't buy sticky notes until she unfreezes the budget."

"Whatever will you do? How will you keep yourself

entertained?" She flipped to a clean sheet on her legal pad. "How much did they cut from my project?"

"You have a thousand dollars and change left in the special project budget and whatever is left in your maintenance budget."

"But I'm in the middle of the project. The office can't open unless it's finished." Leslie dug through the papers on her desk for the last bill Mark had given her. She had been paying each week for the work done. She compared what she had paid with his estimate. She couldn't finish the project with the money she had left.

"You can't open. Well, isn't that interesting." Chuck snickered into the phone. "You're not getting any more money."

Leslie slammed the phone into its cradle. A thousand dollars! She couldn't even pay Mark through the end of the week. She couldn't open for the tax season with the office in its current state.

She grabbed a troll snow-globe and hurled it against the wall. It made a satisfying pop when the glass shattered and the base thudded to the floor. Water and sparkles dripped down the wall.

She slumped against her desk and rested her head in her hands. What could she do? No matter what she did, she couldn't finish the project and turn the branch around this year. For the first time, she was afraid she wouldn't succeed, and she didn't like it. She never failed.

She palmed another troll globe and pitched it at the door. The glass crinkled on the tile, but the destruction did nothing for Leslie's frustration. Her stomach felt as if she had swallowed the contents of a lava lamp. How would she finish the renovations in time without money to pay for the work? She couldn't ask Mark to work for the promise she could pay him when she started filing tax returns and revenue started to come in. What if she didn't file any tax returns? Even if he worked for a delayed check, she'd still have to pay for materials up front as part of their agreement.

She shoveled the papers around her desk, looking for her most recent budget versus actual spending comparison. She found the manila folder and tugged it from the bottom of the pile.

She spent the rest of the morning running numbers and scenarios, searching for the option that would allow her to continue the renovation. She plugged numbers into a spreadsheet, but they never managed to give her the difference she needed. At each dead end, she snatched another troll from her desk and whipped it at the wall.

She hefted the rainbow-haired troll and aimed at the door, when Mark poked his head in. She checked the throw and set the troll back on her desk.

"Hey." He glanced at the puddle of glass, water, and trolls on the floor. "Bad morning?"

"*Bad* would be preferable. This is a disaster." Leslie shuffled the papers on her desk halfheartedly, refusing to meet his eyes and trying to ignore the flush of warmth washing over her.

Mark bent down and picked up one of the trolls. It was only an inch high. "These look even funnier when they're dry. You hear from the consultants?" He shifted a pile of papers from a chair to the floor and sat down.

"Worse." She leaned back in her chair again and tipped her head over the back of her chair.

"The IRS?"

"I'd rather be audited by them for all seven auditable years." She flipped her head forward. How could she tell him? Chuck's glee at her predicament echoed in her head.

"Are they going to close the branch?" Mark looked so solid and unshakable in his usual jeans, sweatshirt, and work boots. Maybe he would understand. Maybe he would have an idea. Since she was coming up with a big zero.

"It's much worse." She grimaced.

"I'm not good at guessing games." He smiled, and Leslie appreciated his attempt the lighten her mood. "What happened?"

"The company split. One of the partners took the major clients with him. The remaining partner is circling the wagons, so to speak. She is trying to keep the company afloat by slashing budgets and spending." She massaged her forehead. The migraine that had threatened earlier cranked itself up a notch. "She cut my construction budget."

"How much?"

"I have a thousand dollars left. Any chance you could get the rest of the project done for that?"

Mark didn't say anything. He rubbed his eyes, then snorted.

"Yeah. I didn't think so." She leaned back over the chair again, staring at the watermarks on the ceiling. "I'll try requesting more money. I don't have a choice. I can't open the office like this. They might as well close it now."

"How long?" Mark leaned forward in his seat.

"I'll know by the end of the week." Leslie rubbed her forehead. Pain flashed behind her eyes like a strobe light at a rock concert.

"Do you still need me to answer the phones?"

Leslie closed her eyes and shook her head. Her temples throbbed. "Sorry. It's a place to save money. I won't be able to open at all if I can't figure out how to finish the remodeling. Would you like to throw a troll?" She grabbed a snow-globe and handed it to him.

He took it, then bounced it in the air. She waited for the crash of glass and the splash of water. It didn't come. He caught it and held it in the palm of his hand.

"I've got a couple other small jobs lined up besides Minnie's. I can keep busy for a few days. Get back to me when you know something. I really need this job."

She heard accusation in his voice. "I had no idea this was going down," she defended herself. She pressed her fingers to her temples, hoping the pressure would alleviate the pulsating pain.

Mark stood to go but turned back toward the desk. "You look pale."

"Just a headache. Didn't anyone tell you never to tell a woman she looks bad?" she said, straining to smile.

He nodded. "You look like you're in pain."

She shook her head, then regretted the action. The room wobbled. "I'll be fine."

Mark stood and paused. She was afraid he might come closer. She didn't think she could handle it if he touched her. She'd burst into tears. Concern filled his eyes. She plastered a smile onto her face, and that seemed to satisfy him.

"Let me know when you've made a decision," he said, and he left, closing her office door. The bells slammed against the door, and she winced. He must be more upset than he'd showed.

She pulled out the salary schedule and added the receptionist's wages into her calculations. It helped. She'd only need to cut her arms off at the elbow to finish the project.

She yanked open a lower drawer of the desk and removed a bottle of ibuprofen. She popped a couple of tablets into her mouth and swallowed them dry. She rubbed her eyes and refocused. She couldn't allow a migraine to push her off course.

By the end of the afternoon, she'd found almost enough for a scaled-back version of the project, but she was still short. On the bright side, she could delay seeing Mark and not have to deal with the turmoil of emotions erupting inside her in his presence.

As she locked the front door to leave, she noticed Mark's globe smashed in the wastebasket beside the reception desk.

Why did that make her feel worse?

Chapter Twelve

Mark dipped the trowel into the tray of drywall mud and smoothed it onto the taped seam between two Sheetrock panels. He slid the trowel along the edges of the tape, easing the excess mud out. The trowel slipped, taking a deep gouge out of the mud. Mark swore and threw the tool into his tray of mud.

"What was that?" Bryce called from the doorway. "I've never seen you throw a temper tantrum."

"Speak of the devil, and he appears. What are you doing here?" Mark wiped a glob of mud off his hands, leaving a gray streak across his jeans.

"I saw your truck outside the Lilac Bower and stopped to see how the work was going. I thought you'd be at the tax office today." Bryce glanced around the room. Bare drywall was smeared with mud. Plastic stretched across the room, protecting the hardwood floor from the splatters off the trowel.

Mark tossed the tray to the floor, and mud slopped over the side. At least he'd concentrated on his job long enough to remember the plastic sheeting. "That job's over."

Leslie hadn't sounded optimistic this morning about finding the funds to finish the remodel. He got the impression she didn't care to see him too often either. He'd wanted to give her the neck rub he owed her right then and ease the pain behind her eyes. In a friendly sort of way.

He snorted. He wondered if he could sell that to anyone.

"She fired you?"

"Good as. Some story about headquarters cutting her funding." Mark leaned back from his squatting position and sat down on the floor. "She claims she can't afford me."

"You don't believe her?" Bryce grabbed a paint-splattered chair and spun it around to straddle it and rest his arms on the back. "Sounds reasonable to me. Big companies do that all the time."

"She was so excited about the remodel. She's gotta be pissed at me." Mark scooped the spilled mud back into the tray and mashed it against one side.

"You two seemed to be getting along all right on Friday." Bryce waggled his eyebrows. "Seemed pretty cozy to me."

"I thought so, too." Mark thunked his head against the wall. His heart beat faster at the memory of her body pressed against his. He closed his eyes and willed the pounding to stop.

"Why would she be ticked off?" Bryce pushed his hat over his eyes and scratched the back of his neck.

Mark cleared his throat, stalling for time. If he told Bryce he'd kissed Leslie, he'd never be able to stop explaining. First about why Leslie would be upset, then about the charade, and then the reasons for the charade, and on and on.

"I get it. That always ticks Judi off. She hates it when we do *that*." Bryce grinned.

Mark rolled his eyes. Now Bryce had taken it too far. "It wasn't *that*. Just a minor misunderstanding."

Obviously, Leslie felt differently. And that was his fault. There had been no need for him to kiss her. No need except his own. He'd lost himself in the moment. In having fun on a date with a great woman.

"Doesn't sound minor to me. She fired you, didn't she?"

Mark didn't want to discuss this with Bryce. Bryce always pointed him in directions requiring significant risks. Like when he pointed out how much Mark hated being a maintenance man at the school, and how Mark should start his own construction company. He got Mark all excited about it, so Mark quit the school before he had a clear marketing plan. He had been scrambling ever since.

Not that Bryce hadn't been right. Mark loved building things.

"Her funding was cut?" Bryce asked thoughtfully.

"That's what she said." Mark mashed the mud back into the bottom of the tray.

No way was he telling Bryce about the agreement

with Leslie. Bryce would tell him a deal like that between a man and a woman didn't happen. And Bryce would give him crap.

"Why would she lie?" asked Bryce.

"She's ticked off. It's a good excuse."

Bryce looked around the room. "This is the crappiest mudding job I've ever seen."

"I needed that job. It was a good way to get my name out there." Mark twisted the trowel, carving trenches in the mud. He hoped Bryce wouldn't think he had another reason to be ticked off.

"You've still got this one."

"Yeah, but working for your aunt doesn't exactly create trust in potential customers. They want nonfamily testimonials." Mark shrugged. "It's not the same."

"So get another job. Advertise."

Mark snorted. "Where? The newspaper is three hundred dollars a week, and it only comes out once. I don't have that kind of cash to shell out."

"Any chance you can get Leslie's job back?"

Not if she's ticked at me, he thought. "She has to fix the place, or she can't open. But the central office could close the branch down before that anyway."

"Make her a deal."

"Work for free?" That wasn't feasible. He had bills to pay.

"No. She's got to have something you can barter for. That's how they used to do it in the olden days. The doctor delivered your baby, and you gave him a chicken. Trade."

"Like what? I'm fresh out of chickens."

"What do you need? What kind of deal could you work?"

Mark stabbed the trowel into the mud, smashing it against the side of the tray so it oozed over in globs onto the floor. Just thinking about her made his heart pound. He refused to look at Bryce.

"I've been racking my brain all afternoon. I've got nothing." Mark sliced the trowel under the spilled mud and scraped it back into the tray.

"Whatever. What does your business need besides advertising? You're always complaining about business something or other."

Mark shrugged.

Bryce stood and slapped Mark on the shoulder. "Think about it. If you do her a favor, maybe you'll find out why she is ticked."

"Bye, Minnie," Mark called as he stepped out the door.

"You're leaving so soon? I thought you'd stay for dinner." Minnie came out of the kitchen wearing a flour-dusted apron.

"I got all the drywall mudded in the front room, and I can't do any more in there until it dries." He turned in the doorway and stepped back inside. "Whether I stay for dinner depends on what you're making."

"What would you eat if you went home? Beer and hot dogs? Do you know what they make hot dogs out of? It doesn't matter what I'm cooking as long as I let you eat it." Minnie flourished her spoon like a scepter.

Mark shut the back door and followed her into the kitchen, his mouth watering, as he smelled Swedish meatballs, his favorite. It was a trap, but he didn't even have hot dogs in his refrigerator, and, after his talk with Bryce, he didn't have the energy to put up a fuss.

Minnie's kitchen was a mix of stainless steel commercial appliances, wooden knickknacks, and embroidered linens. Pots steamed on the cooking surface of the eight-burner gas range. A royal blue and white checked tablecloth covered the kitchen table, and stoneware salt and pepper shakers sat in the middle. A place was set on each side of the table.

"What are you trying to finagle out of me?" Mark asked as he pulled open the door of the oven and breathed in the savory smell. A tray with a clean plate, a cup of chocolate pudding, and a bottle of water sat in the middle of the island.

"Shut that!" Minnie scolded, swatting his knuckles with her spoon. "You'll let all the heat out."

Mark let the oven door spring closed and helped himself to a soda from Minnie's fridge. "What happened to all your beer?" He popped the top and took a long drink.

"Had to bring it to the library. We couldn't have a Ladies' Night Out without adult beverages. It's against our bylaws."

"You have bylaws?" Mark set his soda beside the sink and washed his hands, drying them on the towel hanging from the refrigerator handle.

"You have to be a bona fide organization to use the meeting room at the library," she said, looking down her nose in a regal manner.

Mark shook his head. The Ladies' Night Out group boggled his mind on clear thinking days, and today he was nowhere near the top of his game. He pulled a chair out from the table and sat down, holding his head in his hands.

He had been slightly off balance since kissing Leslie on Friday. He hadn't meant to kiss her. He hadn't intended to. Hadn't even considered it a possibility. She was a friend. A partner in his plot to undermine the Library Ladies. And then he'd lifted her out of his truck. He'd had no choice. He'd done it.

The kiss had thrown him like no other. He kept going back to it, reliving it. While applying mud to the seams in the drywall, he would discover his trowel dripping mud onto the floor as he remembered the softness of her lips, the scent of her hair, and the way her body had pressed against his.

There'd be a lot of sanding to do tomorrow.

"Here." Minnie shoved a plate of meatballs in front of him.

Mark grabbed a fork and stabbed a meatball, shoving the whole thing into his mouth. "Delicious as always, Minnie."

Minnie sat down across the table from him and propped her chin on her hands. Steam rose from the plate in front of her, but she made no move to eat.

After his fifth meatball, Mark asked, "Aren't you eating?"

"How'd it go Friday?"

"I knew there'd be strings attached to the food." He wiped his mouth on his napkin.

"I'm just making conversation." Minnie unfolded her napkin and placed it deliberately in her lap.

"Why don't you ask Leslie? She lives here."

"I haven't seen her. I think she's avoiding me," Minnie said with her fork poised above her plate. She pointed at him. "Why would she be avoiding me?"

"Nothing happened," Mark muttered, and he dug into his meatballs. He'd better eat quickly. Give Minnie less time to interrogate him.

"You wouldn't say nothing happened unless something did. And you especially wouldn't use that tone of voice," she lectured, waving her fork at him.

"What tone?" Mark asked, trying to act innocent.

"The adamantly denying one," she replied, piercing him with a stare that would put terror into the hearts of grown men.

Mark sighed. "We went to the race and for drinks with Bryce and Judi."

"How'd it go?" Minnie pushed her plate aside. She focused entirely on him. He didn't know how long he'd be able to hold her off. Really, the government should hire her. Minnie was an expert interrogator. No one could withstand her intense stare for long. Especially if they'd been softened up by her cooking.

Mark mashed his last meatball into the pile of gravy-laden mashed potatoes. "How'd what go?"

"Bryce's car," she said sarcastically. "What'd you think I meant? What'd you think about Leslie?"

"She didn't howl at the moon, if that's what you're asking." Mark tore a steaming roll in two. "Do you have any butter?"

"For goodness' sake. I know she's not crazy. I want details!"

"Butter?" Mark asked, holding up the roll. Minnie looked as if she wanted to grab him by the scruff of the neck. He liked being on the power side of a conversation for once.

"Details first." Minnie pursed her lips.

"You're not getting any." He bit into the roll. The bread melted in his mouth. Only butter could make it better.

Minnie's face brightened. "That's what I wanted to hear. I knew you'd like her. Butter's in the fridge."

Mark gave her a skeptical look. "It's not about liking or disliking." He set his fork beside his empty plate. "I don't want you thinking something might come of this." He wanted to rave, and he knew he should for the sake of the charade. But it didn't feel right, because the feelings were real and too new to share.

"What, me?" Minnie placed her hand on her chest as if shocked. "I only want your happiness."

"Then leave me alone," he snapped. "You don't need to set me up with every woman in town."

"I have done nothing of the kind." She shook her head slightly.

Mark arched an eyebrow at her. He was almost sorry about his tone. Almost.

Minnie pushed a meatball around her plate. "There are several women I have *not* set you up with."

"When you haven't, Yvonne or Edith or one of the other Library Ladies have."

"I have no idea what you're talking about," she said, but she wouldn't meet his gaze. "I wanted to know if you had fun, that's all."

"You didn't ask Leslie?"

"I haven't seen her since Friday night. I haven't seen her come home tonight yet."

Mark glanced at the clock. It was well after eight. "She's not home yet? She usually leaves the office by seven."

"I haven't seen her come in." Minnie stacked their dishes together and carried them to the sink. She scooped several meatballs and poured them onto a plate along with a dinner roll and garlic mashed potatoes. "I'll make a tray for her. Would you carry it up for me? My back's been bothering me, and I don't want to lift something and climb the stairs."

"Minnie," he said, warning edging his voice. "You said you weren't going to do this. Why don't you ask Leslie if she wants anything?"

"I didn't see her come in. Besides, she's so obsessed with her job, she forgets to eat. She won't remember she's hungry until she gets home and falls into bed. You just have to run upstairs and put the tray in her room."

Mark watched himself adjust the plates on the tray. What was he doing? "It'll be cold by the time she gets home."

"I'm sure she'll be home any minute now. I've got these covers for the food, and I've warmed the plates. It'll stay warm for a half hour."

Mark knew he should refuse. He knew he should leave the tray on the counter and go home. This was another one of Minnie's ploys. In fact, it was the same one. The one where Leslie opened her door wrapped only in a towel.

Pale, smooth skin glistening from her shower and the curves he'd only caressed in the dark when he kissed her. The feel of her body sliding against his.

He grabbed the tray. Leslie wasn't there anyway. He'd deliver the tray and go.

Anticipation shimmered inside him with each step. He wanted to see her. To see if he could find those curves beneath the boxy business suits she wore.

He climbed the stairs slowly. If she was there, she'd take the tray and close the door. She didn't want to see him. She'd fired him.

Mark knocked on the door. No one answered, so he tried the knob. Minnie should have given him the key. He'd have to go get it. The knob turned easily in his hand.

It wasn't locked? Leslie wouldn't leave the door open. City girls didn't do that. He pushed the door open and surveyed the room. Empty. He placed the tray on the table, noting the bathroom light was on.

He moved to turn it off but stopped at the pile of clothes at his feet. Black heels, a black skirt, a cream silk blouse, panty hose. A trail led straight to the bathroom.

He should leave. Walk out the door, down the stairs, climb into his truck, and go home. Take a long, cold shower.

He stepped over the pile toward the bathroom door.

Water rippled and gurgled.

She had just taken a bath. A vision of iridescent bubbles and smooth limbs sprang into his head. He should leave.

He placed his hand on the bathroom door. Anticipation pulsing through him, he pushed the door slowly open.

Steamy fog clung to him, enveloping him in warm haze. His gaze locked on the chaise lounge, where Leslie relaxed, her head propped against the curved arm of the chair. Her hair was piled haphazardly on top of her head, and her eyes were closed. Her entire body except for one foot was hidden under a thick terry cloth robe.

He should leave.

He couldn't move. He stared, breathless.

Fine curls of hair clung to her forehead.

He reached down to smooth one away from her face. His fingertips glided across her damp skin. At his first touch, her eyes sprang open, and she gasped.

"What are you doing here?" She grabbed for the collar of her robe.

"I owe you a neck massage," he said huskily.

"I was only joking." She shook her head almost imperceptibly.

"I never joke when I'm betting."

Chapter Thirteen

He trailed a finger along the side of her neck, his touch cool against her heated skin.

Leslie watched him out of the corner of her eye, debating whether she should end this now. The relaxation she'd gained from the Jacuzzi fled the moment he touched her. A neck massage sounded wonderful, the exact thing she needed after the Chuck's bombshell.

Mark motioned for her to provide room for him on the chaise lounge. She swung her feet to the floor, and he sat beside her. He pressed the fluffy collar of her robe against her shoulders, then kneaded his thumbs in circular motions along the back of her neck.

Leslie opened her mouth to say something, but as the tension eased, she forgot what it was. Her muscles melted. The anxiety oozed out of them. She closed her eyes, relishing his touch. This was the best massage she'd ever had.

He threaded his fingers into her hair, making her purr with relaxation. His caress trailed lightly down her neck and across her shoulder blades. With a slight touch, each tightened muscle softened.

Never had a massage been so effective. The stresses of her day were gone. Troubles faded behind the stroke of Mark's hands on her shoulders. She didn't even remember what the problems were. She could hardly remember her name.

She knew she should say something, but she didn't know what. She couldn't find the words. She appreciated his gesture. Mark seemed to know how to ease her worries, to drive her problems from her mind and replace them with other tempting thoughts. Right now, the only thing she could think about was his hands.

How'd he do that?

If she had been home, she'd have left the office for a sandwich from the coffee shop and a pack of Rolaids. Then she'd obsess over her spreadsheet until the night security kicked her out.

Mark's touch intensified, dissolving months of stress with each stroke. His fingertips were rough from working with wood, constructing things with his hands. Each movement built an unnamed desire within her. A desire that challenged her ambition for success at work. She could feel each fingertip as he kneaded her neck and shoulders. She relished his strength. She felt him shift behind her, and his finger traced the side of her ear.

"I've got to go," he said, his voice ragged.

"Mark?" Leslie said, her voice barely a whisper. Her

eyes flicked open. She sat up. Cool air from the bedroom flooded the steamy bathroom. "Mark?"

She heard her bedroom door slam closed.

Leslie spent the next morning wrestling with her budget and compiling the requested reports. The data didn't look good, but she couldn't change it. The sales for the branch had been declining steadily. Corporate clients had drifted away, and individual tax returns gradually diminished. She could only make her projections as positive as realistically possible. Massaging the numbers to make them look better wouldn't score any points with the consultants.

Staring at the wall and contemplating Mark every few minutes didn't help either. She'd drift away from her reports, reliving Mark's caresses. His abrupt departure still embarrassed her. She could only imagine what he thought. How had she let herself get so carried away? She'd had a total Calgon moment. What was happening to her? Since she'd been sent to Carterville and Mark had almost fallen through the ceiling on her, she hadn't been herself. She'd lost her level head.

She fantasized about Mark. She couldn't seem to remember the simplest things, such as her and Mark's bet. That the neck massage didn't mean anything beyond the payment of that debt. That he'd delivered it when she needed it most—well, that had been a coincidence.

Her computer beeped at her, dragging her away from her disconcerting daydreams. She clicked open the e-mail and saw another request for additional funding denied. Shaking her head, she switched the screen to her remodeling costs spreadsheet.

Delaying the project interfered with her and Mark's agreement to fool the Library Ladies. They wouldn't be together during the day. Unless they went on dates every night, the Ladies would intensify their schemes.

She tapped her fingernails against her laptop. Another problem for the list that kept on growing.

She couldn't open the branch without finishing the renovation. The drywall was half-finished and the floors bare. They hadn't thrown out all the desks yet, but the waiting room chairs were gone. Customers wouldn't stand while their taxes were done; she couldn't fill out an EZ form that quickly even with a computer. Which she also didn't have yet. She only had her laptop, and she hadn't had time to load the newest software updates. She couldn't cut anything else from her budget, and she couldn't raise any more revenue until she started billing for the tax returns. Individual tax returns were the bread and butter for this office. She needed to be ready for the season. If the office wasn't ready, the consultants wouldn't need an excuse to close it. She'd have done it herself.

She hoped the consultants would take her plans for the branch into consideration.

But if they closed the branch, where would she move within the company? As long as it was far away from Chuck, she didn't care. She'd rather be demoted to the mailroom than see him daily. Even the weekly phone calls she received were more contact than she wanted. After he'd stolen her promotion, she never wanted to see his face again.

Maybe another junior partnership would open up, but she knew that dream would have to wait. She'd have to repair the damage Chuck had done and work her way up the corporate ladder again. Assistant manager at a larger branch would be her next step—if she proved herself here. And that meant keeping the place open.

She reached for the folder with her marketing ideas and scanned her list to see if any could be implemented without diverting money from the renovation. She had written them planning for the next year's season. Now she needed them for this year's, if the branch stayed open that long.

The front door jangled. She shoved the folders aside and hurried into the hallway. Mark stood in the entryway in khaki trousers and a light blue button-down shirt under a dark brown leather jacket. The collar was open, revealing the ribbing of a white T-shirt. Under his arm, he clutched an overstuffed manila envelope.

"Hi." She smiled, hoping it wasn't overly bright. Excitement and embarrassment bubbled through her. Just seeing him made something inside her ease open. Something that had never been open before.

Mark didn't make eye contact. He studied the walls, his gaze roving over the unmudded drywall. He shifted from foot to foot. "Were you able to restore any funding for the renovation?"

Leslie shook her head. If he could to stick to business, so would she. "I've worked the budget every way I can. I'm five thousand dollars short every way I figure it." She crossed her arms in front of her and shrugged her shoulders. "I'll come up with something. I just haven't found it yet."

Mark nodded. "I could really use the job for advertising and referrals."

"I'm sorry it's taking me so long. I'm trying every angle I can. I'll still be a reference for you." She clenched her fingers tightly around her arms to hide her frustrated trembling. She had let him down.

"It wouldn't look good if I haven't finished the job." He shifted the manila envelope under his arm. "Can we talk? I have an idea."

She stepped to the side and gestured to the office. "Let's go somewhere with chairs."

She turned and walked down the hallway, conscious of Mark's moving behind her. She fought the impulse to stop and ask why he'd left so abruptly last night. Instead she walked into her office and sat behind her desk. She folded her hands on top of her desk and waited for him to speak. He sat in the chair opposite her, wisely choosing the sturdy one.

Mark opened the envelope and pulled out a haphazardly folded wad of paper. A couple of receipts fell to the floor. He bent over and scooped them up.

"What's all that?" she asked, inching up to peer over the edge of her desk.

"My business papers."

Leslie's jaw gaped open. "You keep everything in an envelope?"

"It seemed like a good idea when I started. Keep it all together. I planned to do something else with it but didn't have time. I just kept stuffing things in here."

Leslie nodded. "Let me take a look."

Mark passed her the envelope with the papers stacked precariously on top.

"Do you have a computer?" she asked, carefully unfolding four receipts cemented together.

"No, not yet." Mark crossed his ankle over his knee. "A couple of jobs fell through, and there went my extra cash."

Leslie winced but pushed the guilt aside. It wasn't her fault her funding was cut. "You're going to need one soon. It'll make keeping track of everything a lot easier."

"Only if I spend time entering the information."

"True." She pushed the pile back into something resembling a stack and tried to shove it back into the envelope. "It will, however, make tax time much less of a headache. You'll have all the reports you need at the click of a mouse. You won't have to file for extensions, and there'll be less chance for errors or audits. You'd even be able to track expenses by jobs to see if your bids are keeping up with actual costs."

"I hoped you could help me with that." He paused. "In exchange for finishing the project. I don't have any cash to pay an accountant to help me."

"I'd be taking advantage of you. There's far more money involved in the renovation than what I would charge for doing your taxes and setting up a computer file." She finally succeeded in stuffing the papers back into the envelope. She bent the little metal tabs and closed it. "I would be willing to do this as part of it, but the difference is too great."

"Not to me. I've been trying to get this done since I started the business. I'm either too busy with work or too short on cash to buy a computer and software. I wouldn't even know where to start. If you did it, it'd be right from the start."

"I won't have a problem getting this done before the tax deadline. But I can't make up the whole difference with this. Doing all your accounting for two years wouldn't make up the difference. Could we scale the project back? What things need to be done to open on time?"

Mark glanced toward her office door as if trying to see the project again. "The drywall and the flooring, for sure. The partitions could wait. We could salvage a couple of chairs, but that doesn't cut costs much." He shrugged.

"What if we split the project in two?" Leslie asked, tapping her pen against her lip.

"How do you mean?"

"Just finish off the reception area. Close off the back office area for now. I won't need it this year anyway."

Mark leaned back in his chair. "That would cut your cost almost in half. You can always do the rest of the work later."

Leslie nodded slowly. This was the solution she was looking for. Money'd still be tight, but she'd be able to open on time. "Does this work for you?"

"Definitely. I get the prestige of a commercial job. People'll see my work. And getting my books in order won't hurt either."

"People won't see it if I can't get them in here." She glanced at the marketing notes on her desk. "That's another problem I need to solve."

"You'll think of something. Try talking to Minnie. She's always got some crazy scheme for advertising the

Lilac Bower. She wanted to buy one of those mini blimps and fly it around the figure-eight arena. Then she found out how expensive they were." He tapped his fingers against his leg.

Leslie's gaze stuck on his hands. The scrapes across his knuckles, the chipped nails, and the purple circle under the nail of his thumb. Her thoughts wandered to the feel of those fingertips on her shoulders and neck. Her breath hitched, and warmth flooded her cheeks.

"Maybe I'll pick her brain this evening." She scratched a fingernail against the metal tab closure. Even though the envelope carried a solution, it still came with set of problems. She'd be more involved in Mark's life. How would she remember to keep up the charade when she could be falling in love with him? She'd spent too much time this morning reliving the massage. If he was around all the time, her daydreaming would only get worse. She couldn't let her thoughts stray every few minutes. These distractions wouldn't help get any work done.

If she agreed to this, she'd have to remember that any flirtatious behavior was part of their agreement. She couldn't let herself get involved. As soon as things turned around here, she'd move on. She was already tangled up with Mark and the Library Ladies and this town. Would she be able to separate what was real and what was a charade? She looked up at Mark. He studied her intently.

She'd have to.

"I'll do it." She placed the envelope on top of her To Do pile and grinned at him. Whatever the cost to herself, it was the only way to get the branch open.

"Great." Mark smiled. For the first time since he'd sat down, his shoulders relaxed from their rigid posture.

Her own tension eased. She'd never thought of trading services. The branch could open on time. She even felt more optimistic about the consultants' evaluation. They would see her improvements.

Mark slapped his thighs, and before she knew what happened, he'd moved around the desk. Spinning her chair toward him, he grasped her chin between his thumb and forefinger. He kissed her on the lips. Leslie's eyelashes fluttered and threatened to close in contentment. So many good things all at once. When he moved back, he looked into her eyes. The brief contact of their lips made her heart pound.

"I'll get back to work this afternoon," he said as he left the office. "Let's have dinner tonight to celebrate the rebirth of the project. I'll pick you up at seven."

Leslie nodded in response and waved, too overwhelmed to find words. She leaned back in her chair, not sure she could sit up straight if she wanted to.

Chapter Fourteen

Leslie pressed another sticky note against the side of her computer screen. Lime green and hot pink notes scribbled with marketing ideas circled her screen and covered her lamp. She opened another spreadsheet on her computer and started compiling numbers. Once she had her reports done, she could prepare for customers, assuming she could find a way to attract them.

She went to the kitchen for a cup of coffee and returned to stare at the notes. Brainstorming was easy, finding a feasible idea more difficult. She pulled the notes off the screen, read them, and tossed them into the trash. They were too expensive or too crazy; none of them would work. She tore the last note from her screen, intending to crumple it with the rest of the bad ideas, but the idea had merit: *Create Buzz*.

It was cheap. She could talk to people. She had to find

the right people. People who liked to talk to other people. She knew exactly where to find them.

And, after all they had put her through, they owed her.

She picked up the phone and paused. Would asking for help only encourage them? She lowered the phone. Probably, but what choice did she have? She cradled the phone against her shoulder and dialed Minnie's number.

"Are the Library Ladies meeting tonight? I need help."

"No, our next meeting isn't until Friday," Minnie answered. "But we can arrange an emergency meeting. I'll see you at five."

Leslie hung up. Things were clicking together. She'd be back at the central office in no time. She could gush about Mark for another hour to get her career back on track.

The phone rang, and Leslie picked it up on the second ring, confident her life was moving forward until she heard the answering voice. The consultants. Every cell froze.

Had they made a decision? Her stomach started to flutter. The reports weren't ready.

"There are some things missing from your personnel file."

Leslie forced herself to breathe slowly and calmly. Her brain searched for what it could be. She came up blank.

"You've had performance reviews?" Mr. Black asked over a rustle of paper.

Leslie didn't need to think about that one. "Yes. Two a year. Mr. Hanston did them. I received glowing reports and a merit increase each time."

Mr. Black coughed. "Yes. We have documentation of

the pay raises but not the reviews. Do you have any idea what may have happened to them?"

"No. Mr. Hanston made copies and gave one to me."

"Do you still have your copies?"

"Yes. But I don't understand."

"We'll need to see your copies."

"I can fax them or e-mail them. Which would you prefer?" Leslie scribbled a note on her calendar, her pen poised for their answer.

Mr. Black sniffed. "We need to see the originals. We need proper documentation on each employee so we can make informed recommendations to the remaining partners. They are concerned about the quality of employees after Mr. Hanston's departure."

"What does that mean?" Leslie frowned at the phone. All of the accountants Mr. Hanston hired were hardworking, meticulous, and responsible.

"We're particularly concerned with the employees he hired. There have been several discrepancies in their personnel files."

"Mr. Hanston hired me," Leslie said aloud to herself. It didn't make sense. Why would there be any concern about employees Mr. Hanston had hired? Unless this was another of Chuck's plots to get ahead.

"Yes. That is why we're giving your file particular scrutiny." Leslie heard him scowl over the phone. "When we see your documentation, we'll be able to sort out this mess."

Leslie blinked rapidly at the phone. "What mess?"

"Certain employees received unmerited promotions and benefits, hurting the productivity of the company by

putting unqualified people in key decision-making posi-
tions. Until we review your evaluations, we won't know
whether you are part of that group. Your promotion to
branch manager was rather sudden." He cleared his
throat.

"It came as a complete surprise to me as well." The
understatement of the year. "I can assure you I'm well-
qualified, and I'm giving this position one hundred and
ten percent."

"Yes. Hmm." She heard papers shuffling. "I'll expect
you at one on Thursday with your evaluations?"

Leslie agreed. Two days wasn't much time, and she
had a mountain of things to finish, but if she didn't jump
when they called, she'd be out of a job for sure.

Leslie hung up the phone. How could they think her
transfer was undeserved? She shook her head. If Chuck
was behind this . . . she'd soak his underwear in jalapeno
hot sauce. If she could bring herself to touch it. She
shuddered at the thought.

She stared at the note on her calendar. What had happened to her evaluations? Why weren't they filed with hu-
man resources? Hanston was meticulous. Someone had
stolen them. Chuck? Jalapeno sauce was too good for
him.

Yvonne and Edith greeted Leslie at the door of the library, handing her a glass of punch even before she slid
her coat off.

"We're so glad to see you," Edith said, grinning and
hanging her coat for her. "Minnie said you needed our
help. No matter what it is, we'd be delighted."

"We'd love to help you in any way we can," said Yvonne, patting her on the shoulder.

"Thank you." Leslie let the fruity liquid soothe her frazzled nerves. The women stared at her expectantly, their hands paused in the middle of patchwork stitches and scrapbook trimming.

"I need help with marketing."

Several women exchanged winks. Had Minnie already filled them in? Leslie explained how she needed to turn around the tax office. She was spending every last penny making it comfortable and welcoming with the latest technology for filing taxes and getting refunds more quickly. As she neared the end, she noticed that the women seemed much less excited. Would they turn her down?

"Do you have any questions?" she asked the sober faces.

"This isn't what I expected." Edith shook her head. "When Minnie said 'marketing,' I thought you wanted a makeover."

"I think we can do this," Minnie said, giving Leslie a thumbs-up. "It'll benefit our community, and isn't that part of what we are trying to do?"

"Benefit our community? How?" Yvonne asked.

"Continuing to have a corporate branch of Hanston and Boyd in Carterville adds prestige to the community," Leslie explained. "We'll be the first to file taxes electronically in town. If the branch does well, we'll hire more employees, and that means more jobs for local people."

"Leslie said we could get our tax refunds in less than three weeks. Remember how long it took your check to get here last year?" Minnie added.

"That was the post office's fault," Yvonne said, picking up her scissors. "They always mix up my address."

"When you file electronically, your refund can be direct-deposited. No post office." Leslie raised her glass. Empty. When had that happened?

"You've sold me," said Dinah.

"Yeah. If you're making a commitment to the community, I'm in," Betty agreed.

"The only way for the branch to stay here is if this tax season succeeds." Leslie outlined the corporate upheaval. "If we don't meet my profit predictions, the branch will be closed."

Several of the women grimaced.

"Are you staying?" asked Yvonne, studying Leslie over the rims of her glasses.

The Carterville branch presented some real challenges, and she was learning a lot, but she'd never achieve her dream of being a CEO here. Mark's face flashed into her mind. She shook it away. Just because she wished they could be more than friends didn't mean she would stay because of him. That was pretend. Just to keep these women off her back.

"I am committed to being here as long as the branch needs me," Leslie hedged. It would only need her until she got her promotion.

"We'll help you out. You'll have the busiest tax season on record," Yvonne said finally.

"Thanks so much. This means a lot to me," Leslie said, relief flooding through her. The branch would have a chance.

Minnie hurried over and gave Leslie a tight hug. "Now hurry home and get changed."

"Changed for what?" Leslie drained her glass of punch.

"Mark said he was taking you out tonight." Minnie pushed her toward the door.

Leslie was glad she'd swallowed, because otherwise she would have spit all over Dinah's scrapbook.

Leslie struggled as Minnie tried to stuff her arms into her coat. Leslie had completely forgotten he'd asked her to dinner tonight. "I forgot. It's been a busy afternoon." She stood up quickly and swayed a little. The punch seemed extra strong.

"Well, get going, then." Minnie shooed her out the door.

Leslie left her car keys in her purse and hurried down the block to the Lilac Bower.

Chapter Fifteen

L eslie grimaced at herself in the mirror. How did Judi make jeans look good? On Leslie, they looked as if she'd stolen someone else's body. A curvy one. Leslie's butt looked as if it had ballooned two sizes in her new jeans. Why had she let the salesgirl talk her into them? She should know better than to take fashion advice from anyone with more piercings than body orifices. She kicked off her shoes and started to unbutton the jeans. She reached for her tailored wool trousers.

A knock at the door interrupted her. She quickly redid the buttons and opened the door.

Mark whistled. "Nice jeans."

"You think so?" She glanced back at the mirror, smoothing her hands over her backside. "You don't think they make my butt look weird?" She slammed her jaw shut. How strong *was* that punch? She'd never ask anyone that.

She met his gaze in the mirror. He wore a plaid flannel shirt and dark navy jeans and exuded masculinity. The speech she'd given herself about how they were just friends obviously hadn't worked. She tore her gaze away and grabbed a pair of black pants off a hanger. "I'm going to change."

"Why?" Mark said, crossing the room. He gently touched her arm. "You look fine. I know better than to answer any variation of the 'do I look fat in this?' question."

"Huh?" Leslie said, licking her lips. Mark tugged the pants from her grip and tossed them onto the chair.

"Always answer 'do I look fat in this?' with 'I've never seen you look more beautiful.' My dad taught me that." He opened the door to her room. "It was the cap to his 'birds and the bees' speech."

"That was part of his sex talk?" Leslie adjusted the bottom of her sweater over the waist of her jeans, anxious for something to do with her hands. She didn't trust them to behave in her usual dignified manner. They might smooth the errant lock of hair on Mark's forehead or test the warmth of his flannel shirt.

"He said if I ever wanted to get any, I wouldn't ever tell a woman she looked fat." Mark grinned, and Leslie laughed. He snatched her coat from the bed and held it up for her. She slid her arms into the sleeves, leaning back slightly as he lifted the coat over her shoulders. She started to inhale the scent of sawdust that always clung to him, then caught herself. If she didn't remind herself about the charade, she'd have fallen in love with him by now. She shoved her feet into her shoes. She had to keep the mood light and not dwell on the direction her heart was traveling. She'd never drink the Library Ladies' punch again. She doubted alcohol was the only extra ingredient. She wouldn't put it past the Ladies to concoct an aphrodisiac.

"So, do I look fat in these jeans?" Leslie teased, placing her hands on her hips and turning from side to side.

"Are you fishing for a compliment?" Mark winked at her.

"Possibly."

"What if I told you that . . ." Mark coughed. "What if I told you those were the sexiest pair of jeans I've ever seen?" He'd thought she'd be cute if she ditched the stiff suits, but he wasn't prepared for the way denim caressed her curved hips.

"I'd say you were finagling for a way to get out of telling me the rest of your setup stories." Leslie grabbed her purse and pulled her hair out of her collar. It tumbled down her back in soft brown waves. Mark couldn't recall seeing her hair down.

"Then you'd definitely be wrong." He closed the door behind them.

Mark followed her down the stairs and out to the truck. He opened her door and reached for her waist.

"No," she said quickly. "I've got it." She placed her right foot in front of the seat and stepped up, grabbing the handle over the door and swinging herself into the vehicle. She plopped into the seat and grinned at him.

He grinned back, disappointed he didn't get to touch her but glad for the excellent view of her backside. He walked around the vehicle slowly, willing his body to calm down. Every nerve fired like a welding rod. And he hadn't touched her.

"You don't seem like a jeans kind of girl," he said as he pulled onto Main Street.

"Bought 'em last weekend. I should take them back. They look awful. They're not me." She propped her elbow against the door and leaned her head on her hand.

"They may not be your style, but they look damn hot." Mark could have bitten his tongue in half. Why'd he say that?

Leslie's gaze whipped in his direction. "You're kidding."

"Watch the eyes of all the males when we go in." He shifted into park. "They'll be glued to you."

"Whatever."

Mark shook his head. Leslie had no idea how great she looked. Most women he knew flaunted their attributes. In every other situation, he'd seen Leslie rise to the challenge with confidence. She marched toward her goals, and she had those consultants eating out of her hands.

This Leslie was completely different. She was vulnerable, needing reassurance.

He parked at the restaurant. He hurried out of the Suburban and had his hands out for her before she could jump down from the seat. His hands slid inside her jacket. Through the soft cashmere of her sweater, he could feel the warmth of her skin and the soft curve of her waist. He couldn't resist pulling her close, inhaling the coconut scent of her shampoo. His hands inched down her hips. He hooked his thumbs into her belt loops and tugged her against his body.

Then his lips were on hers, tasting the fruitiness of the punch, the warmth of her mouth. He pressed his fingertips against her hips, holding her against his own. He relished how the concave of her waist flowed into the convex of her hip.

He gasped as her arms wrapped around his neck, her fingers threading through his hair. He trailed his lips down her neck and found the throbbing of her pulse there, matching the rapid pounding rhythm of his own.

The door of the restaurant opened, and loud voices echoed across the parking lot. Leslie pulled away, breaking the spell. Cool air snaked between them.

They stood apart, their chests heaving, their breath floating in warm clouds around their heads. Leslie fidgeted with her hair and kept sending nervous glances at the group across the parking lot.

Time to rein it in, lover boy, he told himself.

"Shall we go in?" Mark asked when he found his voice.

Leslie tucked a lock of hair behind her ear and nodded.

They headed for the restaurant, the only sound the snow crunching beneath their feet. Mark reached for the door, but Leslie placed her hand over his.

"Why'd you do that?" Her eyes shimmered in the low light, tempting him to touch her again.

A hundred answers lingered at the tip of his tongue, but none seemed right. He settled for "Huh?"

"You kissed me when no one was watching." He saw the confusion in her eyes but couldn't sort out what she'd said from the invitation he wanted to see.

Mark blinked.

"There was no one to put a show on for," she insisted. "I know we have a deal, but . . ."

Then he understood. Their charade. He turned toward the door and tugged it open. "I couldn't help it." If he looked at her now, they'd never eat.

Mark led her to a round booth where you slid in from either side and met in the middle. The Naugahyde creaked as they settled into their seats. The restaurant was lit with colored glass chandeliers, giving the place a warm glow.

The waiter came by for their drink orders. Mark ordered a beer, and Leslie debated for a minute before choosing lemonade. She'd had enough alcohol already.

After their kiss in the parking lot, she needed a conversation topic that would remind her why they were pretending to date. If she didn't keep that in the forefront of her mind, her heart wouldn't survive the night.

"How about those setup stories? How many are left?" Leslie asked.

"Three, I think." Mark scratched a fingernail along the edge of the label on his bottle.

"They'd better be good, because I could use the distraction." Leslie took a long drink of her lemonade.

"The consultants called, didn't they? Are they closing you down?"

Leslie flinched at the thought. "They didn't say yet. It sounds like headquarters is in damage control mode. I have to go to Chicago on Thursday to turn in my reports." She drew an *L* in the condensation on the bottle.

"Are you nervous?"

Leslie traced an *e* and an *s* before answering. She

hadn't thought about it. "It's more hoops to jump through. I've got all the paperwork ready." She smeared the letters into a large drip. "Something could still go wrong, but I don't know what."

Mark placed his hand over hers. The warmth and roughness of his callused hands comforted her. As if his hands had survived tough things. She remembered the relaxation of his hands on her neck and felt herself leaning toward him.

The waiter placed a plate of deep-fried onion rings in front of them, jerking her from her daydream. She grabbed her napkin and unfolded it in her lap. Leslie reached for a ring and bit a hole through the side. She scooted an inch or two away from Mark, eager to match the physical distance with the mental distance she needed.

"How'd you get into accounting?" Mark leaned back and stretched his arm across the back of the booth. He twirled a lock of Leslie's hair around his finger.

"I was captain of the Junior Investors Club in high school and found I had a knack for numbers."

"Junior Investors Club? What'd you do? Sit around picking stocks? Comparing mutual funds?"

Leslie cleared her throat. "If I could've invested real money in my portfolio, I'd be a millionaire. It was good experience. I've already earned a healthy nest egg."

"Why didn't you go straight to Wall Street and make the big bucks there?" His fingertip brushed her neck.

She resisted the temptation to lean into his hand. "I want to own my own company someday. That way I will know how the decisions I make will affect people. Hanston and Boyd offered all that with the possibility of promotion based on merit, or so I thought."

"I didn't know what I wanted to do until about two years ago, when Bryce convinced me to start a construction company. It sounds like you've known since you were a kid."

Leslie nodded. "I want to own my own company someday. Preferably a big one." Leslie took a sip of her lemonade.

She smiled at him. He might have flinched, but she wasn't sure. The dim light hid his expression.

The waiter delivered their entrées. Leslie flattened her napkin across her lap and sliced up the chicken in her salad.

"Tell me about the other women the Ladies tried to hook you up with," she prompted as she stabbed a forkful of lettuce.

Mark nodded as he chewed. When his mouth was clear enough, he said, "This lady wanted me to come out for a repair project. Turns out she'd loosened the hinges on her bedroom door and needed it fixed. Five minutes, I was done with the whole thing."

Leslie dipped a piece of chicken into her dressing. "Sounds pretty normal to me. I wouldn't have known how to fix a hinge."

"She spent the entire time leaning over me, patting my arm and gushing over how strong and manly I was."

"Did that distract you too much to finish the job?" Leslie teased.

"There wasn't anything to distract me with." He shook his head.

Leslie tugged at the collar of her sweater. "So that errand was a bust." She stifled a laugh.

"Well, it wasn't, and the setup didn't work out either." Mark munched a French fry.

"You didn't pursue it because her chest wasn't big enough?"

Mark studied his plate. "That sounds awful."

"If it's true, it's kind of shallow." Leslie took a drink of her lemonade. Mark winced. "Why'd you take off?"

"I didn't run. I fixed her problem. I was there to do repair work, not meet the future Mrs. Schultz."

"You could have talked to her for a minute. Maybe she's nice. Give it a chance."

"I didn't want to." He shrugged.

"It's the same with all the women. You never give them a chance."

"There wasn't a spark."

"Spark?"

"You know what I mean." He sighed. "Electricity. Chemistry."

"Is this the blond and big boobs thing?"

"No. Well . . . no. You've never felt a connection with someone the moment you met? The almost instant knowledge that this person is someone you want to know better? That this person would incite you to take a chance?"

"I've never heard it described like that," Leslie mused aloud, studying Mark closely. His face was serious and intent. She wished he felt that way about her.

"Chemistry?" he asked.

"Love at first sight."

"It's not love." He shook his head.

"You didn't describe lust either. If it was lust, you would have been all over the Barbie replicas."

"I don't know how to describe it. It's something that says, tell me more." He picked the onion off his hamburger. "Maybe it's the first step to love, and I haven't seen anything in the setups that made me want to take another step."

"Because the situations were artificial?"

"I don't think the feeling can be contrived, but if it was the right woman, it'd work. It wouldn't matter how we met."

"So why me?" Leslie leaned forward, propping her chin on her hand.

"Why you what? We aren't dating." Mark shoved his empty plate across the table.

They weren't, she reminded herself, but it still stung to hear him say it. She finished her lemonade and set the empty glass on the table. They weren't dating. They were friends helping each other out. So it shouldn't hurt to hear it.

But it did. Sharply.

"That's not what I meant," she said, hoping her cheeks weren't flushed or, if they were, he couldn't see them. "Why haven't you tried the charade before? I'm sure any of them would have welcomed the opportunity."

"No one would have respected the agreement the way you have. They'd have pushed the boundaries whenever they could. Our agreement serves you as much as me. You said you didn't want any distractions from your work."

Leslie nodded. Her words exactly. Although *he* seemed to be pushing the boundaries.

"What happened before you left Chicago?" Mark crossed his arms over his chest and slouched in the booth.

Leslie blinked at the abrupt change of subject. "I got 'promoted.' " She drew quotes in the air.

"You had a boyfriend or something, right?" Mark shifted in the booth to face Leslie.

"Not even close." She shivered. "I had a disagreement with a co-worker. He didn't take it well and recommended me for this transfer."

"You can make it more colorful than that. I've told you some very good stories."

"There's nothing colorful about it. He may have used some colorful language when I stumbled upon him and one of the partners in the supply closet during the Christmas party. Now that I think about it, they were wearing holiday underwear and party hats, so I suppose that was colorful."

"See? You were holding out on me. What could be more fun than festive underwear? What did he do when he saw you?"

"He begged me not to tell anyone. Blah, blah, blah. When I arrived at work Monday morning, he told me to report here by nine the following morning. Happy New Year to you." She raised her glass in a mock toast.

"What an ass." Mark shook his head.

"Not much I can do about it. Who can I report him to? The other partner left. Besides, it's my word against theirs, and I'd come out looking whiny. I have to make the best of it."

The waitress brought fresh drinks and cleared away the empty plates. A band was setting up on the small stage, and other customers moved chairs into a semicircle around it.

The band leader made a quick introduction, and several people cheered. They played a slow song, and several couples moved out to the dance floor, holding each other closely as they swayed to the music.

"Dance with me." Mark slid out of the booth and extended his hand to her.

She took it and slid around the other side. "Just part of the deal, right?" She followed him to the dance floor. She placed her hand on his shoulder. He took her other hand in his and held it close to his chest.

Mark and Leslie swayed slowly to the music. Leslie stiffened at the lyrics about 'When I hold you close, I know I've found the one. The love of a lifetime.' They were supposed to be pretending, not dancing to a song newlyweds played at their reception.

Mark eased her closer, humming softly. Leslie closed her eyes, allowing herself to enjoy the feel of Mark and the refreshing scent of sawdust and aftershave she could only describe as Mark. She could pretend for a few moments. She relaxed, drifting through the song, swaying without thought to the endearing words, "When the time is right, we'll find a way to make it last forever." When the song ended, Mark kept her in the circle of his arms.

"Let's go for a drive," he said before they sat down at their table, his voice husky and low.

Chapter Sixteen

L eslie grabbed her purse and hurried down the hall to the restroom before she and Mark left. As she emerged from the stall to wash her hands, another woman with long blond hair, tight jeans with Playboy bunny silhouettes on the rear pockets, and a T-shirt that fit like a second skin stood in front of the mirror fussing with her hair. Leslie pumped antiseptic soap into her palm and turned on the faucet.

"Are you here with Mark Schultz?" the blond asked, adjusting her bra and her T-shirt so a full three inches of skin showed in the deep V-neck.

Leslie twisted the knobs closed and dried her hands under the air drier. "Yes. Do you know him?"

"We went to high school together." The woman dug in her purse for a lipstick and, upon finding it, coated her lips in a glossy red. "I'm Tara." She flashed a super-red smile at Leslie.

"Leslie." Leslie held out her right hand, and Tara grabbed it with both hands.

"It's great to meet you. I haven't seen Mark in for-ever," Tara said, as if she were doing a cheer at a football game. "Are you guys married?"

Leslie tucked her purse under her arm. "We're friends."

"Oh. You won't mind if I say hi, then," Tara squealed as they walked back to the tables.

Leslie watched Mark's eyes snap to Tara like magnets to metal. Suddenly she felt like mist in the wind. Mark had forgotten all about her. He completely focused on Tara and her push-up bra.

"Tara?" he asked, looking stunned.

Leslie wondered how he recognized her; he had barely spared a glance at Tara's face.

"Yeah. It's me." She threw her arms around his neck.

Would she spell her name out, too? Leslie thought. She probably had a cheer for it. "Give me a *T*!" Kick to the side. "Give me an *A*!" Jump in the air. And a grand finish with a wide spread-eagle, toe-touching jump. Leslie rolled her eyes.

"You look great," he said as Tara stepped back.

Tara slid her hands down his arms. "You've been working out." She giggled.

Mark got a goofy grin on his face. "Yeah." He shrugged. "Some. What are you up to? You back in town?"

"I decided to come home for a while. See my mom and all. It's the off-season, so I've got some time off."

"Off-season?" asked Leslie, wanting to slap Tara's hands away from Mark.

"I'm a cheerleader for arena football."

Leslie nodded. She'd have never guessed that one, she thought sarcastically.

"I'd forgotten." Mark said, shoving his hands into his back pockets. "How long will you be in town?"

"A few weeks. We should get together for drinks some-time." She patted his arm. "You know, catch up." She laughed, her professionally whitened teeth sparkling in the dim light. "If you're not busy." She winked at Leslie.

"No. I'm not busy. What's your number?"

Tara scrawled her number on a napkin, drawing a smi-ley face next to her name. Mark folded the napkin and stuck it into a back pocket.

"I'd like to go home now," Leslie said. "I'm not feel-ing very well." In fact, she felt like gagging. Wasn't this how all men reacted? And after all that crap about sparks and chemistry. It didn't matter that she and Mark weren't really dating; that display was disgusting.

Mark promised to call Tara later and took Leslie home. He didn't say much in the truck, and Leslie didn't encourage him.

She needed to get out of these jeans and remind her-self who she was. Maybe a cup of black coffee and a hot shower would clear her head. A woman like her didn't attract the attention of men like Mark. How had she al-lowed him to get by her defenses?

She tried to hop out of the truck before Mark could get around to lift her down. She didn't want him to touch her and make the pain of the charade more unbearable. The illusion had been painfully obvious when he greeted Tara. She needed a napkin to wipe away his drool.

Her feet hit the ground, and her purse slipped out

from under her arm. The snap popped open, and the contents spilled across the cement as Mark opened the door wider.

"I was coming to help you down."

"I can manage." She knelt to scoop up the contents of her purse and shove them back into gaping bag.

Mark bent to help her. He grabbed a little black book and turned it over. He stood up and opened the front cover.

Leslie glanced at him and froze. She had forgotten about that. *The Encyclopedia of Romance* she'd found in her bathroom.

"Gimme that." She lunged for the book.

He held the book just out of her reach, catching her arm before she landed on the pavement." 'Gimme' gets nothing."

Leslie jerked away from him. "Please give it back." She held out her hand, hoping he wouldn't read the title. After witnessing his meeting with Tara earlier, she didn't need any further humiliation tonight.

"What is this?" He flipped the book over and tilted it toward the streetlight. He turned a few pages and stopped. He looked at her and then glanced back at the book.

"I was going to throw it away." Leslie dropped her hand and crossed her arms over her chest.

"That would be a shame. There's some useful stuff in here." He turned a couple more pages.

Useful for what? Him and Tara? Ugh. She didn't want to think about it. "It's not mine. I found it." She bent down to retrieve the rest of the contents of her purse.

He arched an eyebrow at her. "Page seventy-three is particularly appealing."

"Someone left it in my bathroom." Leslie shoved some receipts into her purse, refusing to look at the page he held open for her.

"At the office?"

"No. Here. I didn't want Minnie to think it was mine, so I was going to throw it away at the office." She clicked the snap of her purse shut and started for the bed-and-breakfast. "You can keep it. Just don't tell anyone where you found it. I don't want anyone to think it's mine."

"Minnie." Mark nodded as he unfolded a dog-eared page. He whistled.

"Minnie what?" Leslie spun around.

"Minnie left it in the bathroom." Mark turned another page and slowly tilted his head to the side, studying the image.

"What? It's Minnie's? That's a mental picture I didn't need."

"No. Not like that." He shook his head, his eyes still focused on the book. "It's part of her new marketing scheme. Make the place more attractive to younger people. She wants to attract guests who don't fall asleep before *Wheel of Fortune*." He turned a page. "Why were you going to throw it away?"

"I thought a previous guest had left it, and I didn't want Minnie to be upset by it. I was going to toss it into the office Dumpster. I forgot about it."

"Minnie's more liberated than that." He snapped the book shut. "How long have you been carrying it around?"

"Since I moved in." Leslie sighed.

Mark winced. "I'm sure Minnie checked for it every

time she cleaned. She probably thinks you're memorizing it."

Leslie hid her burning cheeks behind her cool fingers and muttered an unladylike word. Could she do anything else stupid tonight?

"No wonder Minnie wanted to set us up."

"I never looked at it." Why hadn't she tossed it when she had the chance? Leslie held up her hands in protest. "Give me the book. I'll put it back in the basket." She held out a hand.

"This might be fun." He flashed a page to her.

Tara's face and T-shirt flashed in front of her eyes. If he wanted to do that, he could call Tara. Then it would fulfill all his fantasies.

"No thanks." She tore the book from his hands and stuffed it back into her purse. She hurried into the bed-and-breakfast and up to her room. She pulled the book out of her purse so she wouldn't forget to hide it in the bottom of the basket.

Minnie stuck her head out of her room as Leslie reached the top of the staircase.

"We made a few phone calls, and the marketing campaign's underway."

"Uh, thanks. I appreciate that." Leslie tried to hide the book behind her purse. "I'm heading off to bed."

"Alone? Someone needs to get that boy into gear." She rolled her eyes and disappeared inside her doorway.

Getting him into gear wasn't the problem, Leslie thought. *I'm not the woman*.

She didn't know if Minnie had seen the book or not,

but Leslie couldn't wait to get it out of her hands. She tucked it under the extra bath towel at the bottom of the basket and sighed.

People weren't this crazy in the city.

Chapter Seventeen

When Leslie unlocked the door to the office the next morning, the phone was ringing. An unusual occurrence that usually meant bad news. She hurried to answer it anyway, dumping her coat and briefcase on the chair.

"Hanston and Boyd," she said breathlessly, thinking the name of the company might have changed, but it was still the name on the deteriorating awning on the front of the building.

"Is this the place that does taxes electrically?" The voice on the other end scratched.

"Yes, we can file your taxes electronically," Leslie said, smiling to herself about filing taxes with the electric company. She rolled her chair to her desk by hooking her foot on the base and pulling it.

"Then sign me up. I like newfangled things."

Leslie arranged an appointment and penciled the customer's name and phone number on her calendar. Her

183

first customer. She smiled. The morning was looking better. She'd barely replaced the phone in its cradle when it jangled again.

She hung up from that call with four more appointments and the promise of two more. The woman claimed she would get her other two children to come as well.

The phone rang all morning. The second line rang moments after she picked up the first. Her calendar quickly filled with names and phone numbers. A whole week full of appointments. The Library Ladies were phenomenal. If this continued, she'd have to hire help.

The phone rang again. This time Judi's voice was on the other end.

"I'm having a Super Bowl party on Sunday. You want to come? It's going to be the same people who were at the race and a couple of others."

"Is Mark going to be there?" Leslie scribbled a note on her calendar.

"Of course. Speaking of . . . how did last night go?"

"As in?" Her pencil hovered above the paper.

"I heard you were slow dancing and looking pretty cozy."

"News travels fast here, doesn't it?"

"The streets are short and traffic is light. Is that why your line has been busy all morning? So, what gives? Is the truth as spicy as the gossip?"

Considering that the evening had ended catastrophically with Tara's appearance and that little black book, Leslie didn't want to revisit it.

"I asked the Library Ladies for help with marketing.

I guess they were busy. My schedule is filling up," she said, trying to distract Judi.

Judi sighed. "If you do business taxes, schedule me in there somewhere. I need help getting all my deductions for my home office."

"Business taxes?"

"I have a consulting firm. I help school districts and day cares set up training for teachers and parents. I facilitate various groups to set up procedures to meet state standards and qualify for state and federal aid."

"Wow. I had no idea. You run this all yourself?" Was this the same Judi who cleaned strained peas out of Boppy's high chair? She ran a consulting firm?

"I wanted to set my own hours and spend as much time as possible with Boppy. I get to use my teaching degree and spend quality time with my son. This works great. I'm my own CEO." She laughed over the phone.

Leslie scrawled Judi's name on the calendar and hung up the phone. Judi had her own business. Leslie had assumed that Judi was a stay-at-home mom, but she was in charge of her own business. Something nontraditional that allowed her to do all the things she loved. Leslie couldn't help but feel jealous. Judi had what she wanted in life; Leslie still searched.

The momentary silence was interrupted by a knock on her office door.

"Hey, you are here!" Mark called, pushing the door open.

Electricity shot through her body at the sound of his

voice. "It's where I work." She flipped open her laptop and punched the power button. Keep this professional, she told herself. His reaction to Tara meant nothing to her. It didn't affect her in the least.

Too bad, it did.

"Minnie called my cell. She said she tried to call you all morning, but your line was busy and she couldn't get through. She was afraid you passed out and knocked the phone off the hook."

"The phone has been off the hook. I've had customers calling all morning." She held up her calendar. "Look at this." She gestured to the columns filled with penciled names and phone numbers.

"Guess you're going to need a receptionist again. You won't have time to do taxes if you're always answering the phone."

Leslie nodded. "I'm also going to need the remodeling project done. I can't have customers tripping over ladders and sitting on drywall buckets."

"I can't wait to get to work." Mark scanned the walls. "I'll be done by the end of next week."

Leslie felt his steady gaze on her. She grabbed some papers from a stack and pretended to study them.

"I'll be in Chicago tomorrow," she said quickly, hoping to divert any suggestion on his part that they should end their agreement. With the project almost done and Tara in town, he was probably itching to get out of it. "If you need to get in touch with me about anything, here is my cell number." She slid a business card out of her calendar and handed it to him.

He pulled his wallet out of his back pocket and slid

the card into a pocket. She wondered if the napkin with Tara's number was tucked in there.

"This the meeting with the consultants?" He tucked his wallet back into his jeans.

The phone rang again. Leslie nodded as she answered it and scheduled another appointment. "I'm definitely going to need a receptionist. At least while I'm gone."

"I would offer, but I have some serious drywalling to do." He winked and nodded to the reception area.

Leslie laughed. He could ease her tension with such a small gesture. "I know. Do you know anyone willing to work cheap?"

"I talked to Tara this morning. She's looking for something temporary while she's in town. She's great with people."

Leslie tried not to grimace. She didn't want to believe her sudden urge to vomit was because Mark hadn't even waited twenty-four hours from their heart-stopping kiss to call Tara. What happened to the forty-eight-hour rule about calling women who gave you their phone number? She shouldn't be surprised, picturing Tara's T-shirt.

She didn't have time for personal issues. She had a business to run, and she needed someone this afternoon. She'd never get her reports done with the phones ringing like this.

"What's her number?"

Mark took the napkin out of his wallet and read the numbers to her.

Leslie scribbled them on a sticky note. She wondered how long before the napkin disintegrated from being pulled out of his wallet.

"Thanks. What'd Minnie want?"

"She said a couple of Express Mail envelopes arrived for you, and she thought they were important," Mark said as he headed for the reception area.

Leslie called Tara and arranged for an interview in half an hour. She hurried over to Minnie's and got back in time to see Tara walk into the office.

Tara wore a gray tweed skirt and jacket with a silk blouse. Her hair was wrapped in a neat chignon at the base of her neck. The bulkiness of her coat did nothing to hide her oversized implants.

Leslie sighed. She had to give Tara credit for trying. She hoped Tara wouldn't distract Mark.

Mark, unfortunately, was easily distracted. He stopped applying mud to the drywall seams, and it dripped unheeded off his trowel and onto his boots as his gaze tracked Tara's progress.

Tara said something and laughed, continuing toward Leslie with a graceful sway of her hips. Leslie led her to the office, trying to ignore Tara's saying she'd see Mark later.

Leslie asked some rudimentary interview questions and was pleased with Tara's answers. Tara handled herself well and spoke clearly and smoothly.

Leslie asked her if she had any experience with being a receptionist.

"I did have a job talking on the phone, but I didn't make appointments or anything like that." Tara looked uncomfortable. "It was a multiline phone system, so I'm comfortable transferring calls and talking with customers." She took a deep breath. "I'm trying to get into something

I can tell my mother about. She doesn't approve of the cheerleading either. I was very good on the phone."

The phone rang. Leslie snatched up the receiver and scheduled the appointment. She had to hire someone, she thought as she hung up the phone. She wouldn't be able to get the office ready to open if she was on the phone all the time.

"I'll need you to answer the phones and schedule appointments."

Leslie showed her how the appointment book was arranged and gave her a list of questions to ask and information to give the customers. She situated Tara on the opposite side of her desk until the receptionist area was ready. The phone rang, and Tara was off and running. She handled each call expediently and politely.

Leslie spent the rest of the afternoon finishing her reports. She listened to Tara every now and then to make sure she avoided gossip. Other than a few "Yes, I'm back in town's" and "Sure, call me at home's," Tara stuck to the instructions Leslie had given her. She gave Tara a key when she closed up.

Tara would work out fine on the phone. At least for this week, Leslie told herself. She could always hire someone else later.

Chapter Eighteen

L eslie collated her reports and evaluations into neat piles and binder-clipped them together at the small table in her room at the Lilac Bower. She packed the reports into an expandable plastic folder and snapped the elastic band into place. When she tucked it into her briefcase, she noticed the Express Mail envelopes.

She'd forgotten about them in her rush that afternoon. She extracted one and tore it open. A thick stack of insurance forms and retirement brochures tumbled into her lap. It looked like a benefits package. She sifted through the papers for a letter but found none. She ripped open the cardboard strip on the second envelope. Enclosed was a letter on the letterhead of Hanston & Associates. The letter announced that the new firm was pleased to offer her employment and was signed by Ed Hanston himself. He'd even scrawled a note below the typed letter, saying he couldn't wait to meet with her. She should contact them at her earliest convenience to discuss the details of the position. A complete benefits package would be sent separately.

Leslie stared at the letter in shock. Had Ed taken her missing evaluations? She regarded him more highly than Ms. Boyd and was disappointed that he'd left the firm. She flipped through the preliminary benefits package again. Nothing discussed the position and its responsibilities.

At least, she thought, she'd have something to fall back on if she was cut from Boyd.

Fall back on? She should be jumping at this. Better salary. Better wages. Better work environment. The position couldn't be any worse than what she had now.

But was the position better? That she didn't know, and that must be what was holding her back. She'd have to wait and see what it was like.

Leslie thumbed the number into her cell phone and made arrangements with Ed's assistant to meet with him as soon as she arrived in Chicago. It wouldn't hurt to hear what he had to say.

Leslie pressed the button for the twenty-third floor and the offices of Hanston & Associates, waiting while the elevator accelerated through the intervening floors. Her excitement built as the elevator climbed. This could be her dream opportunity.

The elevator slowed, and the doors hissed open. Leslie smoothed her hair and stepped into the plush reception area. A receptionist ensconced behind a large oak countertop greeted her. Brass adorned the light fixtures and doorknobs. Leslie's heels sank into the padded carpet. Quiet classical music flowed through the room. Classy elegance—so like Ed and exactly what she was aiming for.

"Ms. Knotts is here to see you." The receptionist spoke into the intercom. The oversized double doors behind the desk opened without a creak, and Mr. Hanston emerged. He wore a black suit with white pinstriping. His hair, recently blessed with Grecian Five, glistened with hair oil.

"Ms. Knotts," he said, extending his hand and flashing a veneered smile. "Leslie, how good to see you again."

"Ed." She smiled. "Thank you. You look well yourself. This office is fantastic." She shook his hand firmly, reminding herself to concentrate on this meeting and not dwell on the upcoming one with Ms. Boyd. Once they saw the list of appointments, they'd keep the branch open. She didn't see any other option. The branch was on course to make a profit for the first time in five years. She smiled at Mr. Hanston.

He gestured for her to precede him into his office. The décor of the office matched the reception area. All the chairs gleamed in brown leather.

"Please have a seat." He motioned to an overstuffed chair in front of a low coffee table. "Would you like something to drink—coffee, tea?"

"Black coffee would be wonderful," Leslie said, placing her briefcase beside her chair.

Ed poured the steaming liquid into a gold-edged china cup. He set it delicately on a saucer and handed it to her. He refilled his own cup and sat across from her on a matching sofa.

"I'm glad you were able to meet with us so quickly. I thought Ms. Boyd would have you locked up in that dreadful little office." He sipped his own coffee. "I've followed your career since you started with Hanston and Boyd. In establishing my own firm, I'm creating an accounting firm of the best and brightest young people in the city. Your performance has been exceptional—one of the best I have seen." Ed placed his cup on the coffee table. "I'd like to offer you a position as junior partner with my firm. You'd work jointly with a senior partner on several of our most prestigious accounts. If things go well, as I'm sure they will, you'll have a full partnership within two years." Ed outlined some of the projects she would oversee. "I would also like to place you solely in charge of the Stoddard account."

"The Stoddard account?" Leslie couldn't help gasping. This was everything she had been working toward. A partnership with a respected firm. Influential clients. Multimillion dollar accounts. It was all there. More than the promotion she'd expected when she was exiled.

"You've handled several very difficult clients with extreme care. I have no doubt you will treat Stoddard with the same delicacy and professionalism."

"This is an amazing offer. I could hardly . . ." Leslie stared into her cup of coffee.

"I must say I was horrified when Ms. Boyd sent you out to the Carterville branch," Ed interrupted. "Why she decided to waste your talents there, I don't know. I see no conceivable way of making that miserable place profitable. Better to cut it off and be done with it. I think you deserve something better. Take some time to consider the offer. I don't want you to rush into this without careful consideration about what you want for your future."

Why hadn't she screamed she would accept the position immediately? She couldn't find the words to accept.

Carterville. That was what kept her from accepting. The potential of it. She could make the branch profitable; she knew it. She wasn't wasting her time. The people of Carterville needed her. She was disappointed that Ed didn't see that. Leslie placed her empty cup back on the table.

"I am at a critical point in the project in Carterville, and I'd like to see it through. I'm afraid I can't accept the position at this time. I appreciate the offer and your respect." Leslie stood.

"I'm sorry to hear that. I thought you'd jump at a chance to advance your career. I never thought you'd want to stay out there in that dead-end branch. Ms. Boyd will close it the first chance she gets." He shrugged. "If you ever need a reference, I am available." Mr. Hanston withdrew a business card from the inner pocket of his jacket and handed it to Leslie. "Here is my direct number."

Leslie drove the circles of the parking garage, her unease and agitation mounting with each turn. Near the top, she finally found a parking spot and climbed out of the Civic. She straightened her skirt and adjusted her collar. Pulling her briefcase out of the passenger seat, she took a deep breath and let it out slowly. She had turned down her dream job because she wanted to stay in Carterville? She could hardly believe it herself, but after all the hard work she'd done in the last few weeks, her plans were coming together, and she wanted to see them through.

She had no idea what she was walking into. Her only contact with headquarters had been through Chuck or the consultants. Who knew what was actually going on here? Neither one of her sources was forthcoming, but the interoffice politics here didn't concern her as much as the future of the Carterville branch.

Her agitation eased. All she had to do was convince the consultants that the Carterville branch was turning around, show them her appointment book. It couldn't be easier. She opened the glass door and confidently strode across the tiled lobby.

Chuck met her at the elevator. He was dressed in his usual charcoal gray suit and burgundy tie. His graying blond hair was trimmed short and gelled into tiny spikes on top of his head. Somehow he made a power suit seem as slimy as that of a streetwalker's pimp. How had she been impressed before? Her back straightened, and her teeth clenched.

"Good to see you again," Chuck said. "You look good. Country air must agree with you."

"It's good to be back. Where are Mr. Black and Mr. Brown?"

"In the back conference room. Ms. Boyd's there, too." Chuck led her down an alley between anonymous gray cubicles. One of these had been hers a month ago. They seemed claustrophobic now. While her office at the branch was small and overstuffed with file cabinets, it had a door and was entirely her own.

"How boring is Carterville?" Chuck snorted, brushing an invisible piece of lint off his tie.

"Not as bad as you might think. There are a lot of colorful people in town. They make the quiet evenings pleasant." Her thoughts traveled to the Library Ladies and Mark. Mark made Carterville more than pleasant. If only Tara hadn't shown up. She pushed the thought aside. She couldn't dwell on that now. "And since I work alone, I don't have to worry about a co-worker stabbing me in the back." She faked a smile, continuing toward the partner offices and conference rooms on the far side of the floor.

They stopped at an office door. "This isn't the conference room," Leslie said.

"No. I thought you'd like to see this." He tapped the brass nameplate beside the door. CHARLES SILVERMAN: PARTNER.

"She made you a full partner?" Leslie asked. "Are they crazy?"

"Possibly." Chuck smirked. "Boyd and Silverman Accounting. Sounds good to me. I'm not going to question it. I may be able to hire an assistant when everything shakes out. You interested?"

Leslie ignored him and stepped into the conference room. All the suits at the end of the table stood. The consultants quickly resumed their seats. The table was covered in neat stacks of paper and folders. In the center of the table was a brown plastic tray, stacked with Styrofoam cups, a carafe, and a half empty container of nondairy creamer.

"Please have a seat." Ms. Boyd came around the table

and gestured to a chair in the middle of the table, directly across from Mr. Brown and Mr. Black.

Leslie sat and placed her briefcase on the floor beside her seat.

"We are pressed for time," said Mr. Black, pushing his glasses onto his nose. "We hope to keep this quick. Do you have the papers we asked about?"

"Yes." Leslie pulled them out of her briefcase and handed them across the table. If they were in a hurry, that could only work in her favor. They would surely send her back to work after a quick review of her paperwork. "These are my copies of my evaluations, and these . . ." She withdrew a second stack. "These are the reports you requested."

Chuck took the seat beside her and poured himself a cup of coffee. He held the carafe up to her; she shook her head. Not that she had anything to worry about, she reminded herself. All the reports were in order, and there was nothing in the least worrisome in her personnel evaluations. Mr. Hanston had rated her "excellent" in every category. She'd be on her way back to Carterville in no time.

"Hmm," Mr. Brown said, showing Mr. Black something on one of her evaluations. "Did Mr. Hanston sign off on all your evaluations?"

Leslie shrugged. "As far as I know, he did all of them."

Mr. Brown flipped through all the evaluations. He nodded slowly.

"All of my evaluations have been positive and even glowing in some instances. I don't see what the problem is here."

"They are excellent," Mr. Brown said, frowning. "Just like all the others that have been suspect." He and Mr. Black exchanged glances.

Suspect? Excellent recommendations are suspect? What's going on here? Leslie looked from the consultants to Ms. Boyd and Chuck. They were whispering and flirting and not paying any attention to the consultants.

Leslie rolled her eyes. Chuck was working on keeping his partnership the only way he could.

"I see you've revised your expected sales figures for the upcoming season upward," Mr. Black said, peering at her over the papers through his eye-enlarging glasses.

"Yes, that's correct," Leslie said, folding her hands in her lap. "I've had phenomenal success with my marketing plan. Appointments are rolling in."

"These projections aren't realistic." He shook his head. "That branch can't turn around the way you say."

"Judging by the number of appointments I already have, these estimations may even be too low," Leslie said firmly. Couldn't he read the paper in front of him? She clenched her hands tighter in her lap to keep from reaching across the table and shaking him.

Mr. Brown remained unconvinced.

"They are projections, but in comparison to previous years, this return load is much better. I believe the Carterville branch has potential," she insisted.

Chuck stifled a laugh. Leslie wished she'd taken coffee, so she could spill it in his lap. Unfortunately, barely enough steam emanated from the carafe to cause more than dampness and mild discomfort.

"As you know, the company has split, and we are

forced to take measures to preserve its integrity and unity," Ms. Boyd said. "We also need to stabilize our financial situation with our creditors by eliminating deadweight. The Carterville branch is unprofitable and will—by our projections—continue to be so. We plan to close it as soon as possible. It's a risk we simply can't afford to carry at this juncture."

"The Carterville branch will be profitable this year. You can't shut it down. It'll be in the black by May. Sooner, if appointments continue as I've anticipated."

"We want the branch closed within a week," Ms. Boyd reiterated.

"These people trusted this company enough to let us do their taxes," Leslie persisted. "We can't abandon them. It'll destroy any company loyalty we have in Carterville."

"You'll have plenty of time to inform the customers," Mr. Brown said. "We plan to give them vouchers for other branches. Discounts always make people happy." He folded his hands on the stack of reports.

"There are no branches within an hour of Carterville. You're going to lose all the new customers I worked so hard to get." She paused for breath, her indignation rising. All the things she'd promised the Library Ladies had been chewed up and spit out. They were abandoning Carterville—exactly what Leslie had promised they wouldn't. Leslie stopped abruptly. All these customers had put their trust in her. If she wasn't there, she'd be abandoning them. But where would she be? "What about my job? Is that being eliminated also?"

"Yes, well, it's time we come to that," Ms. Boyd said.

"As all your evaluations were certified by Mr. Hanston, I have no choice. I must ask for your resignation." She paused. "We are reorganizing and want to ensure that the remaining employees are a unified team willing to work toward the same goals and objectives." She sipped her coffee. "According to your evaluations, you've had close associations with Hanston and many of the clients who went with him."

"I worked as a very junior associate on many different accounts during my career here. According to my evaluations, my work was exceptional on all of them. I don't see how that can be grounds for dismissal." Her mind fought to understand what Ms. Boyd had said. Ms. Boyd couldn't be firing her?

Ms. Boyd poured herself another cup of coffee. "We're concerned that this association might endanger the unity of the company. We don't want Hanston head-hunting any more of our employees, so we want to weed out those he may have an interest in before he has a chance to steal them away."

" 'Weed out'? I'm being fired?" Leslie leaned forward in her seat and tapped the table with two fingers. She must have misunderstood. She glanced at Chuck. He was engrossed in carving his initials into his Styrofoam cup.

Ms. Boyd cleared her throat. "I would prefer to call it an amicable separation. We're prepared to offer you a generous severance package to compensate for the abrupt ending of our business relationship." Boyd slid a paper across the desk. "This outlines the compensation we are prepared to offer. Six months salary and health insurance benefits as well as a two-year equivalent payment into your 401(k)."

Leslie pulled the paper toward her and pretended to study the numbers. Stars swam in front of her eyes, and light-headedness washed over her. They were actually firing her? She'd just been offered a junior partnership with Hanston & Associates, which she had turned down to remain at the Carterville branch, and now Ms. Boyd was firing her? She peered through her eyelashes at Chuck, who could barely contain his amusement as he fiddled with the diamond stud in his right ear. If only she could grab a hold of it and twist, that would wipe the smug smirk off his face. She clenched her jaw to keep from gaping like a landed fish.

"There are, of course, some concessions you must make in return for this." Boyd tapped the agreement. "First, you must agree to work for one more week or until the branch business is wrapped up—whichever comes first. During that time you will close the branch office and file any necessary reports. You will also prepare the office building for sale. The remodeling improvements should help fetch a nice sale price."

Leslie stared at the paper, her mind numb. Throw all her plans into the trash can and stomp them down. Then set them on fire and watch them burn. "You trust someone you're firing to do all this?"

"You'll be closely supervised. Besides, there aren't any corporate secrets at the Carterville branch."

"Any other stipulations?" she choked out.

Ms. Boyd took a deep breath. "Second, you must not

work for any of these clients during the next year." She handed her another paper.

"These are the clients who went with Hanston?" Leslie scanned the list. Stoddard's account was listed there.

"Yes, the major ones. Third, you must sign a standard noncompetition agreement."

"So, you don't want me, but you don't want me to work for anyone else either?" This had to be Chuck's idea. She was sure it was when she saw him shift in his seat as if he had ants in his pants. If only they were fire ants, she thought.

"Yes and no. Our main concern is our direct competition. We don't want Hanston's firm stealing any more of our workforce or our clients. The agreement covers Hanston and Associates and four others considered our direct competition. The consultants recommended this strategy for keeping the rest of our major clients with the company. Of course, not all of the account executives who worked with our former clients are being released."

"Only the ones who had close connections to Mr. Hanston," Leslie finished for her.

"During the next week, you will be a considered a full-time employee of our company and will be required to work on closing the Carterville branch and preparing the building for sale. As soon as everything is closed up, we will deliver the severance package."

There was something she'd like to sever—the part of Chuck's anatomy that had gotten him his promotion.

Leslie fumbled for the fountain pen. It felt awkward in her hand. She placed the pen on the paper and scrawled her name. Her fingers moved on autopilot. She slapped the pen down on the paper and shoved her chair back. "Are we done here?"

Ms. Boyd and Chuck stood, holding out their hands for her to shake. The consultants merely nodded.

Leslie looked at the outstretched hands and picked up her briefcase. She turned and left the office with as much poise as she could muster. She wanted to run back to her car and Carterville and pretend this meeting hadn't happened. If only she were at the Lilac Bower, still asleep in her bed.

Chuck's voice echoed down the corridor, followed by Ms. Boyd's scratchy laugh. She hoped Chuck would not follow her to the elevator. She couldn't be held responsible if the elevator doors were to open early and he were to accidentally trip and fall down the empty shaft. Leslie walked to the elevator with her back straight and her face rigid. She wouldn't let them see how shocked and angry she was. She wouldn't make them happier.

She would have liked to throw the coffeepot into Ms. Boyd's face, disgusted by the extracurricular activities she'd used as criteria for promotions. There was no other way Chuck had gotten his name on the letterhead. She forced herself to remain professional. She couldn't believe the consultants were making such poor recommendations. What future did Boyd & Silverman Accounting have with their advice and the leadership of slimeballs?

None of that mattered. She didn't work here anymore. She'd turned down Mr. Hanston's offer because of her loyalty to Carterville, only to be fired hours later. The worst part was that she had worked so hard . . . for nothing.

She pressed the button for the main floor and slumped against the wooden panels as soon as the doors hissed shut. She pulled her phone out of her purse. She needed to rant to someone about the injustice, but who?

Mark. She stood still, staring at the display of her phone.

Shouldn't she want to call someone from the city, a friend from work, first? No one came to mind.

She pressed in Mark's area code and stopped. Why would he care that she'd been fired? They weren't anything. They were pretending to be something. But he didn't need her around anymore. He had Tara now, the epitome of his fantasies.

Leslie cleared the number. She wouldn't call him. She could talk to him when she got back to town. She pushed the buttons to play her messages and placed the phone to her ear. There was Tara.

"Hi. Just calling to say the phone's been ringing off the hook. I had to start scheduling in March. Mark started painting. The color is fabulous, and the carpet arrived. It's great. I wanted to thank you for giving me a chance. I know you didn't have a lot of choice because you were in a hurry, but anyway, thanks. Good luck with your meetings, and Mark says hi." Tara giggled and then disconnected.

A little smile curved Leslie's lips. Working with Tara was like having her own cheerleader, but Tara's enthusiasm did little to dispel her disappointment.

March. According to the records of previous years, there hadn't been this many appointments for the whole tax season, let alone two months. And it was all for nothing.

She stopped walking in the middle of the sidewalk. People hurrying by jostled her, but she barely noticed. Leslie stamped her foot. None of it would happen. She'd never get to see how her plan worked.

Leslie reached for her phone. She should call Tara and tell her to stop taking appointments. She dialed the number, but a busy signal buzzed in her ear. She shook her head. It could wait until tomorrow.

Chapter Nineteen

She arrived back in Carterville well after the office closed, so she drove straight to Minnie's. Her head ached from all the ranting she had done on the drive back. Her eyes felt bloodshot and dry from the exhaust that had been sucked into her car while she sat in a traffic jam outside Chicago.

All her energy had drained out of her hours ago. She couldn't comprehend all the ups and downs. She'd turned down her dream job, only to get fired from her current one. Maybe some sleep would help. Rubbing her eyes, she pulled her keys out of the ignition and dropped them into her purse. She heaved herself out of the car and pushed the button for the trunk release. The trunk lid popped open, and Leslie reached for her suitcase and briefcase.

Someone reached around her and grabbed the handle of her suitcase. She spun to face Mark.

"What are you doing here?" She stumbled backward into the bumper of her car.

"I was working on one of the bedrooms and saw you pull in. I was starting to wonder if you were going to get out of the car or sleep there." He grinned.

"It's been a long day. I wasn't sure I could move." She rubbed her eyes and smiled weakly. How did he do that? He'd made her smile when she had nothing to smile about.

"The meetings were that good, huh?" He followed her up to her room, carrying her suitcase.

"An emotional roller coaster." She unlocked her room door and tossed her briefcase onto the chair. She kicked off her shoes and unbuttoned her jacket. Mark set her suitcase next to her briefcase.

"Are they closing the branch?" Mark closed the door and leaned back against it.

Leslie pulled her jacket off and dropped it on top of her briefcase. After today, the purple of the room seemed soothing, the lace doilies like stepping into the comfort of her grandmother's living room.

"They call it 'reorganizing,' but it's the same thing." She pressed her fingertips into her temples. "I'm supposed to get the branch business shut down and the building ready for sale."

"What about your position? Are you moving back to the central office?" His voice was quiet.

Leslie's stomach clenched at his question. She didn't want to say she'd been fired. She wasn't sure her tongue could form the words. She pulled the pins out of her hair, releasing some of the tension in the back of her head.

She fluffed her hair loose and closed her eyes. If she said it, it would actually be true.

"I have been informed I am persona non grata with the Boyd half of the company because of my close association with the Hanston half. My employment ends as soon as everything here is closed up."

"They can do that?" Mark pulled her to him and wrapped his arms around her.

Her body melted into his, relishing the support and comfort. She tentatively slid her arms around his waist. "To Ms. Boyd, I'm a liability to what's left of her company because Hanston may want to head-hunt me. In fact, Hanston offered me a junior partnership, but I turned it down because I wanted to see the project here through." Tears stung her eyes. She pulled away from Mark and tried to blink them away before he could see them. She didn't cry about anything.

She grabbed a tissue and blew her nose. "Car exhaust always aggravates my allergies," she mumbled, tossing the tissue into the trash and massaging the back of her neck.

Mark tugged her over to the bed, and she sank down. Mark sat beside her and pushed her hands away from her neck. He caressed the knotted muscles. "Isn't that your dream job? The promotion to get you out of here?" He continued to massage the back of her neck and her shoulders.

"Yeah. I should have taken it. So much for company loyalty." She shook her head. The tension in her shoulders and neck was melting away. She closed her eyes.

Only moments ago, all her muscles were tight enough to snap. Now she was almost asleep.

"It's their loss. If they could see how the branch is coming together, they'd be kicking themselves." Mark leaned closer to her, and she could feel the warmth of his breath on her neck. He squeezed her shoulders.

"How is the office coming? I have to get it ready for sale." She sighed.

"I've got most of the painting done. The carpet arrived yesterday afternoon. Tara loves it. By the way, thanks for hiring her. She really appreciates it. Her last job was getting her into trouble. She was glad to get a chance at something else, even if it is only temporary."

Leslie didn't want to talk about Tara or think about Mark and Tara's spending the day together. Probably reminiscing about high school.

"Yeah. I didn't have many options. Who does real estate stuff around here?"

All she wanted at the moment was to enjoy his touch and pretend for a few moments that this was something more than it was.

"Edith does, or she could connect you to someone who works with commercial stuff. I'll get you her number tomorrow."

The thought of all the work involved with selling the building exhausted her. She winced just thinking about it.

"Hey, try to relax," Mark said, dragging his fingertips down the back of her neck. "Don't think about it until tomorrow. You don't need to worry about it until then."

"I could use another story. Something to distract me. I haven't heard any funny stories all day."

"How many have I told you?"

"There's got to be at least one left. You haven't told me about the crazy one yet."

"We went on a date, and she started screaming at me. Someone called the police. They would have just escorted her home, but she bit the deputy."

"Did the Library Ladies apologize?"

"Not in so many words, but I've never had more boxes of cookies left on my doorstep in one week," Mark said.

"I can't believe they'd dare to set you up with anyone after that."

"They don't have a conscience. They believe everyone over twenty-five should be in a committed relationship."

Leslie knew she had underestimated the Ladies now. Once they set their sights on someone, they kept at it. No wonder they claimed one hundred percent success. They'd be disappointed when things with her and Mark didn't work out. But now he had Tara. Mark and Tara— that was another thing she didn't need to think about today.

"They should work on Tara. Sounds like she'll be around for a while."

"Thanks again for giving her a job. She appreciates it."

"She said she had a lot of experience on the phone. But in a different capacity." Leslie pulled a pillow into her lap and picked at the lace.

"Yeah, I'm sure the rumors are worse than the truth," Mark said. "She's not the person she used to be." The warmth of his fingers dropped away from her shoulders.

"I didn't say 'rumors.' It's what she told me." Leslie's tone was clipped. "How would I know anything about what she used to be like?"

"She's changed," Mark said stiffly.

"I didn't say she hadn't," Leslie insisted. She'd had enough injustice today.

"She needs someone to give her a chance."

"I have given her a chance." She turned to face Mark. "A temporary one, but I can't help that."

Mark gave her a frustrated look. "Tara's had a rough time. I don't want to see people continue to treat her like a tramp."

Wasn't anything going to go her way today? Now Mark was angry with her as well. Obviously, he cared deeply about Tara, and she didn't have the energy to explain what she meant.

"You know, I'm tired. I didn't mean to imply she was a tramp," she said apologetically. "Perhaps you should go."

Mark left, and Leslie flopped back on the bed. Tomorrow could only be better, right?

She'd lost her job, her office, and her boyfriend all in one day. Her pretend boyfriend, she reminded herself. Could she fault him for defending Tara, an old friend and his possible love interest? She couldn't blame him, but that didn't make it hurt less. She blinked at the sting in the back of her eyes. She wasn't going to cry, was she?

This wasn't worth crying about. Her job was business. It wasn't fair, but it wasn't personal. Then she remembered Chuck's arrogant smirk. It was personal.

He'd enjoyed her being forced out. She suspected it was even his suggestion.

Leslie rubbed a knuckle across her eyes to ease the stinging, surprised to feel tears. She smeared them away. She didn't cry.

Mark could date Tara. Marry her, even. Leslie and Mark were nothing but a ruse. Unfortunately, Leslie knew she had fallen for it. Probably faster and harder than the Library Ladies.

What was wrong with her? She didn't give in to emotional breakdowns like this. She wiped more tears on the cuff of her blouse. She crawled across the bed and pulled the covers up to her chin. She'd allow herself to wallow tonight. Get it all out of her system.

Tomorrow she'd be ready to face the world again.

Chapter Twenty

When Mark walked into the office the next morning, both phone lines rang simultaneously. Tara waved her fingers at him as she spoke to the caller. He placed a cup of coffee on the desk as she jotted notes on the calendar. She mouthed "thank you" as he walked by.

The room smelled of fresh paint and new carpet. The colors—whatever they were—were much brighter than the paneling. He'd installed the carpet squares last night after he left Leslie. He'd even moved a desk into the reception area for Tara. He'd been too agitated to go home.

Leslie's reaction to his defending Tara had puzzled him. But Leslie had said she was tired. It sounded as if she had had a rough day and had a lot to think about.

Since Tara was still taking appointments, he guessed either Leslie had not informed Tara that the branch was closing, or the branch was not closing immediately.

Leslie's office door was closed, but her light was on. He tapped on the door and pushed it open. She was also on the phone. Mark couldn't remember a time when both phone lines had been in use at the same time.

He placed a second cup of coffee on her desk and backed out. Leslie glanced up at him, the expression on her face unchanging before she looked back down at the legal pad she was scribbling on. The renovation was close to being finished. He had to finish the carpet squares along the walls and then do the trim work.

A man in a gray suit and a bright tie opened the front door, holding a cell phone flipped open. His blondish hair was greased into slick spikes. The man turned toward the window, raising and lowering the phone. He was trying to find a signal. Carterville was notorious for random dead spots in cellular service. Tara scowled at him with her arms crossed.

"You can't go in there," she said. "Ms. Knotts is on the phone."

The man huffed and placed his fists on his hips. "Ms. Knotts is expecting me," he insisted.

Mark didn't like how the man said Leslie's name—as if the word tasted of spoiled fish. He looked wiry, but Mark thought he could take him.

"What seems to be the problem here?" Mark stepped behind Tara's desk.

The man half turned and snapped his phone shut. He tucked it into an inside jacket pocket. "You must be the reason."

"The what?" Mark crossed his arms in front of his chest. He was sure he could take him.

"The reason Leslie was so eager to get back here. I thought she would stay in town for a couple more days."

Mark rested his hand on the hammer hanging from his belt.

"Actually, I'm Mark Schultz, Schultz Construction. I'm the general contractor for the renovation project." He extended his hand. Mark's best guess was that this was Chuck. And that fact gave him the urge to growl. He squeezed Chuck's manicured hand until he felt his knuckles mash together. The slimeball.

Chuck gave him a sickly smile.

The click of Leslie's heels echoed down the hall. Mark turned toward her as she entered the reception area.

"What's going on? I heard voices."

Mark glanced at Leslie, who looked as if she wanted to slice Chuck into minced tuna.

"Why are you here, Chuck?"

Chuck adjusted the sleeves of his suit. "Ms. Boyd sent me to oversee the sale of the property."

"She didn't trust me to take care of it?"

"Part of my job is to oversee all the branch closings." Chuck tugged his shirtsleeves until they had all seen his diamond cufflinks.

"She sent you out here to babysit me?" Leslie shook her head. "You must not have much to do."

"Babysit? Exactly what services would that involve?" Chuck's gaze traveled over Leslie's body.

Leslie crossed her arms in front of her chest and fidgeted with her collar.

Mark stepped closer. *Slimeball* was too good.

Chuck glanced at Mark and flinched. He turned back to Leslie. "Is there someplace we can talk? Alone?"

Leslie tilted her head toward the office. Chuck gave Mark a curt nod and scooted down the hallway.

"What a schmuck," Mark muttered.

"I thought so, too." Tara straightened some papers on her desk. "You looked as if you wanted to chew him up and spit him out, then drive over him a couple of times with your truck."

"Did I?" Mark glanced down the hall at Leslie's office door. The idea had appeal. His hand clutched his hammer again.

"So, what's going on between you two? I asked her, and she said you were friends."

"We are," he said, still staring at Leslie's door.

"Right." Tara looked skeptical, but the phone rang before she could say more.

Mark shook his head and went back to the loading dock.

Leslie allowed the door to shut behind her. Crying herself to sleep last night had done little for her mood this morning. Her eyes felt swollen and clogged with grit. She walked slowly to her chair behind the desk. Chuck had chosen the only other chair in the office with arms. It might have looked like the most comfortable chair, but it had lost a caster and wobbled whenever its occupant moved.

He glanced around the office. "What a dump. This place will never sell. I'm here to court any corporate clients."

Leslie tapped a pen against the blotter. She exhaled slowly and counted to ten. It didn't help. She wished the bad leg of his chair would give out.

"Good luck with that." *Why wouldn't that leg collapse?*

"We don't want them to feel we are abandoning them when we close the branch."

"What else would you call it? The closest branch is over an hour away. People around here won't go that far."

"We will service them via the Internet. It will be more convenient. They won't even have to leave their offices."

"Chuck, the clients you're afraid of losing won't use the Internet. If they don't know someone who knows you, they won't do business with you. You're wasting your time here. You've already lost them."

Chuck stared at her as if she had told him people would never want a television in their home.

Chuck scowled at her. "Looks like you know everything there is to know. How many corporate clients are on the list?"

"Exactly zero."

"Zero? Why's the phone ringing off the hook?"

"Those are all individual income tax returns, and they're first-time clients. Are you going to fill out their 1040s by teleconference? If you kept the branch open and established a more permanent manager, this branch would thrive."

"Are you trying to get your job back? With the proper encouragement, I could be persuaded to put in a word with Ms. Boyd." Chuck winked and shifted. The short leg wobbled.

Leslie kept her face calm. She knew exactly what he meant by "encouragement." The only thing she wanted to "encourage" was the leg of his chair to snap.

"You know my aspirations are greater than being a branch manager for Boyd and Silverman, or whatever they're calling it now." Then she had an idea. "I made a list of clients I planned to court. You could go visit them." She pulled the list out of a drawer and handed it to Chuck.

She'd pay money to see Chuck's reaction when he met the guys at the trailer demolition place. Okay, so they weren't actually potential clients, but having them on the list might get rid of Chuck. She hoped when they shot at him, they didn't hit anything life threatening first.

Chuck attempted to stand, and the chair finally tumbled over. He picked himself off the floor and stormed out.

Leslie waited until the bells on the front door chimed before laying her head on her desk. Couldn't anything go her way? Encountering Chuck's inelegant innuendos first thing in the morning was enough to curdle her break-fast. After yesterday's roller coaster ride, she had been looking forward to a day alone with her computer and her reports.

She'd talked to Edith that morning about the sale of the building. She would make arrangements for advertising and an appraisal. Edith said the branch could take a while to sell because the market was slow. If they wanted it to sell quickly, they'd have to price it low.

Mark seemed to be avoiding her as well. She hadn't talked to him beyond the quick questions he'd asked about furniture placement. She didn't know how much longer she could keep up the charade. Sooner or later he'd see that her pretending was anything but. She didn't want him to feel he had to let her down easy. She knew what their agreement was, and it was her own fault she'd allowed him to touch her heart. Somehow, it was worse knowing he'd moved on to Tara.

The one bright spot of all this was the office. No matter what Chuck said, it was exactly as she had hoped. The renovated area was bright and welcoming. They'd had to use the old molded plastic chairs, but otherwise everything looked great. Mark had arranged the reception area with Tara's desk on one side of the door and a row of chairs on the other. At the other end of the room, he'd arranged a desk and a couple more chairs.

The phone rang as she placed the appraisal in the pile of paperwork she had for Chuck.

"Hey. Are you going to lunch anytime soon?" Mark asked through the hollow echo of his cell phone.

"Half hour maybe. Why?" Leslie said, glancing at the clock.

"I'm having car trouble, and I need a ride."

"I can call a tow truck for you." Leslie reached for the phone book.

"I tried, but I keep getting the machine. Mike must be at lunch or something."

"I can leave now. Where are you?"

Mark gave her directions to a back road in the area of the fairgrounds.

"I'll see you in a few," she said, and she hung up the phone. She grabbed her car keys and her purse, calling an explanation to Tara as she hurried out the door.

Mark's directions were good, and she easily found the

street, although she had been concerned when he told her to turn on the corner by the red cow. What if the red cow was in the barn?

The cow, she learned as she swung the Civic around the corner, was fiberglass and standing in front of the Red Cow Dairy.

A couple of miles farther down the road, she found Mark's Suburban parked on the shoulder with the hood up. When she pulled to the side of the road in front of him, he swung the door open and jumped out. He came around to the driver's side of her car.

"What happened?" Leslie asked, lowering her window.

"Thanks for coming out. I'm not sure what's wrong with it. It lurched a little, and then it died. I've never had trouble with it before." He rubbed his hands together. "The heater won't work or anything."

His gaze met hers, and she didn't think he needed a heater. Warmth spread through her body. This was the first time they'd been alone together in days. She'd missed their easy banter and his relaxed attitude.

"You popped the hood," Leslie said, surveying the truck through her windshield. "That's one step farther than I would've gotten."

Mark slammed the hood down and locked the doors of the truck.

"You're locking the doors? I didn't think anyone around here did that."

"I've got all my tools in there. People in this area will ignore a hundred-dollar bill, but they'd walk off with my tools without blinking an eye."

He climbed into the car, and Leslie did a U-turn in the narrow road.

"Where can I drop you off?" she asked, when they got to the stoplight on Main.

"My house. Maybe I can get a hold of someone from there."

Mark directed her through town to the opposite edge. She pulled up in front of a freshly painted farmhouse. The sage green house was two stories with a wraparound porch and delicate scrollwork along the railings and roofline of the porch. Icicles clung to the eaves, but she could imagine sitting on the porch on summer evenings, sipping iced tea and watching the sunset.

"You live here?" Leslie asked, looking at a house that couldn't belong to a bachelor.

"Yeah. I've been working on the interior between jobs. I finished the outside last fall."

"I imagined you living in a studio apartment with an unmade bed and an empty refrigerator." Leslie peered through the windshield at the house. It looked so sweet and comfortable, well worn and well loved.

Mark climbed out of the car. "Don't look into my bedroom, then. Would you like to come in for lunch? Minnie gave me leftovers."

Leslie climbed out of the car and hitched her purse onto her shoulder. They walked up the sidewalk, and Mark pushed open the door. He motioned for Leslie to enter. She stepped around him into an empty room. The floors were hardwood but in desperate need of refinishing. Despite that, the room was pleasant, with several windows lining each of the exterior walls.

Leslie shed her coat, and Mark draped it over the banister. "The dowel in the closet rotted, and I haven't replaced it yet."

The walls of the hallway had faded from what must have been a very vibrant pink. Squares of the original pink dotted the walls, and narrow cracks zigzagged from the floor to the ceiling.

"I haven't done much on the inside yet. Minnie's job and yours have kept me pretty busy the last few weeks."

The next room held a television, a stereo, and a sofa that looked like a dorm room reject. Videos and CDs were stacked haphazardly on the floor next to a television stand composed of scrap plywood separated by cement blocks.

The kitchen was at the rear of the house, and the window above the sink framed a snow-covered field. The cupboards were painted with thick white paint and had handles shaped like fleur-de-lies. Everything else looked original to the fifties, including the metal kitchen table and chairs.

"No wonder the Library Ladies want to get you married off. They don't like the idea of your rambling around here by yourself all the time." Leslie's gaze strayed to the window. "It's a lovely view."

"They're in a hurry for me to fill the bedrooms upstairs as well." Mark draped his Carhart jacket over the back of a chair.

"How many are there?"

"Four and a loft." Mark removed a Tupperware container from the refrigerator and peeled the top off. "I want to merge two of them together, make a master bedroom with its own bathroom.

He stuck the container into the microwave and turned the dial. The microwave started humming and then buzzing. Mark smacked the oven's side with his palm, and the buzzing returned to humming.

"I was thinking . . ." Leslie said as she sat at the kitchen table and traced a finger along its Formica design.

"What's that?" Mark asked, looking over his shoulder as he extracted paper plates from a bag on the counter and shook plastic forks from a cardboard box. He placed them on the table, and Leslie separated them into place settings.

"About our arrangement. Now that Tara's here, it doesn't seem necessary anymore."

"What does she have to do with anything?" Mark asked, leaning back against the counter, his hands on his hips.

"She's more of what you are attracted to, isn't she?"

Why was he staring at her that way? As if she had told him that aliens were climbing through the ceiling.

"I mean . . ." She took a deep breath. "We can still be friends. I don't want to be in the way. I know we had a deal, but I'll be leaving soon. I think we should dump the charade now, and you can ask Tara out. I mean, if you want to."

Mark blinked but didn't stay anything. He punched the release for the microwave door and eased the steaming plastic dish onto the counter. He jammed a spoon into the casserole and placed it on the table.

"Is this about Chuck the Schmuck?" he asked.

Leslie saw her chance. Maybe if he thought she had a thing for Chuck, she could get away without Mark's realizing how hard she had fallen for him. She told herself it was for their own good. They had to stop pretending sometime. Why not now, while Tara—the woman of his dreams—was in town? Leslie knew it would burn like a thousand paper cuts to see them together, but not being with him was going to hurt like heck anyway. It was best to break everything off cleanly. And then maybe her heart would stay whole.

Leslie nodded. "Chuck wanted to change the nature of our relationship, since we won't be working together anymore." She couldn't lie and say she thought it was good idea.

"I see." His voice was flat.

"I should be going." Leslie checked her watch and grabbed her purse. "Thanks for lunch. Hope the truck's okay."

She didn't want to stay and have to explain any more. She didn't want him to know how hard it was for her to remember that his attention to her was fake. He should be relieved anyway. He'd be free to pursue Tara and still evade the Library Ladies. They'd be happier with a local girl anyway.

She grabbed her coat off the banister and threw it over her shoulders. The sawdusty scent of Mark engulfed her. She looked down and saw his scarf wrapped around her neck. Tears stung her eyes. She pulled the scarf close to her face and scurried out the door.

Chapter Twenty-one

Leslie pulled on her new pair of jeans and chunky wool V-neck sweater. Stuffing her feet into suede boots, she decided to enjoy the Super Bowl party tonight. She'd been dwelling on the injustice of her firing for long enough. It was time to stop.

Leslie climbed into her car and started the engine. Her hands dropped from the steering wheel and into her lap. She had been looking forward to the evening ever since Judi called. Mark and Tara would be there, and she'd have to watch their relationship grow, but she was determined to ignore it.

When she arrived at Judi's, the driveway was filled with cars. Mark's Suburban was parked in the driveway in front of the house. Leslie parked behind him and went inside.

Judi greeted her from the kitchen as Leslie walked in. Judi placed a steaming tray of croissants on the stovetop and shut the oven door. "The pregame show's on downstairs. Beverages are here." She gestured to the refrigerator. "And at the bar downstairs. Food is everywhere."

"Do you need any help?" Leslie asked, pushing up the sleeves of her sweater. She wasn't quite ready to face Mark and Tara.

"Actually, yes." Judi looked around the kitchen, then grabbed a bread knife from the counter. Judi handed the knife to Leslie. "Bryce's mom picked up Boppy later than I expected. I haven't split the croissants open yet."

Leslie set to work, slicing the warm bread open.

"The Library Ladies haven't been too bad lately, have they?" Judi asked.

"Minnie hasn't had anyone ambush me while I was in the shower in about two weeks." Leslie laughed. "Maybe they've given up."

Judi stacked the sliced croissants in a wicker basket lined with napkins. "Let's take these downstairs. I have the rest of the sandwich stuff down there."

Leslie followed Judi down the stairs into an open basement. Chairs and a sectional sofa formed a semicircle around a muted big-screen television. Along one wall, tables were laden with sandwich makings, potato chips, pretzels, and cookies. Bryce, Mark, and a couple of men Leslie recognized from the figure-eight race congregated around the bar, where Tara held court, laughing and sipping a drink from a plastic cup. She tapped her fingers against Mark's thigh.

Leslie plastered a smile onto her face, hoping she hadn't flinched at Tara's intimate contact with Mark.

Mark met her gaze, and Leslie smiled back in what she

hoped was a friendly way. She couldn't decide what emotions Mark's expression held. He didn't seem content.

"Oh, Leslie. I'm so glad you came." Tara hopped off her stool and rushed over to Leslie. "These boys are boring me." She giggled loudly.

Leslie doubted the "boys" were doing anything of the kind. The "boys" gave a collective groan of outrage.

"Whatever." Tara winked at them. "All they want to discuss is football stats, and unless it concerns Tom Brady's butt, I have no interest."

"This is a Super Bowl party," Leslie pointed out. "Football is the point."

"I suppose." Tara shook her head and pulled Leslie to the food table. "I'm dying for some Cheetos." Tara grabbed a handful and started munching. "I wanted to thank you again for giving me a chance. A lot of people see the blond hair and the implants and write me off."

"I'm sorry it's not permanent. With the office closing, unfortunately . . ." Leslie shrugged. She took a handful of Cheetos and placed them on a napkin. "You're great on the phone. If you need a reference for another job, feel free to put me down."

"Thanks." Tara threw her arms around Leslie. "That is so sweet of you. What are you going to do when the branch closes? Oh, sorry. I got crumbs on your sweater." Tara wiped at the orange dust with a napkin.

"I haven't decided yet," Leslie said, flicking the last crumb off her arm.

"I suppose you'll go back to the city." Tara munched another cheese puff.

"I was thinking about it. I could go to any big city.

There aren't many places around here that have openings for a CPA."

"Probably not. You should start your own company. You'd be a great boss. Ooooh. The game is starting." Tara dashed to the sofa and squished herself between Mark and the man Leslie thought was Noah. Mark scooted out from under Tara, and she plopped down on the couch cushion.

Bryce thumbed the remote, and the emcee announced the kickoff.

Leslie moved closer to the group, eyes on the television. "I thought you didn't care for football."

"Tight pants," Tara said, licking the cheese dust off her fingers. "And the commercials."

"What's your favorite commercial?" Mark asked.

"I like the horses playing football."

"Leslie, what about you?"

"The Monster one from a couple of years ago. 'I want to be stuck in middle management.' Those kids were hilarious," she said, sitting on one of the chairs to the side of the sofa on the opposite side from Mark.

"That's what I thought you'd say," Mark said. He looked at her intently. He sat reclined on the couch with one foot propped on an ottoman and his arms spread across the back cushions of the sofa. He seemed so relaxed and open. She wanted to sit in the circle of his arms like Tara was.

"How would you know that?" she asked, feeling her face flush.

"It just fits you." He stared at her, his face contemplative.

"How about you? What's your favorite?" she asked to deflect his attention away from her.

Mark thought for a moment. "The frogs. 'Bud. Wise. Errr.' Although it's hard to beat 'I want to have a brown nose.'"

Bryce cheered, pointing at the television. "Touchdown!"

"Already? They've only been playing for two minutes." Mark leaned forward, waving his arm over Tara's head and grabbing a handful of M&M's from the bowl on the coffee table.

"Interception. End zone. Boom." Bryce clapped his hands.

"I believe Mark needs to donate a buck to the pot," said Noah.

Mark sighed and shook his head. He tugged his wallet out of a rear pocket and pulled out a dollar bill. He tossed it into a glass bowl on the coffee table.

"What's this?" Leslie asked, after taking a sip of the soda Judi handed her.

Bryce raised his beer toward Mark. "Mark is the only one who thinks the Patriots aren't going to win again this year."

"We agreed to put a dollar in the pot each time a team scores. Mark puts one in when his team scores. The rest of us each put one in when the Patriots score. The winner gets the pot."

"It helps break up the monotony between commercials," Judi said, pulling up a chair beside Leslie.

"I thought you learned your lesson about betting at the figure-eight race," Leslie said to Mark. Then she wished she'd bit her tongue. Why was she flirting with him?

"The punishment wasn't all that bad." He gave her a

look that made her catch her breath. She picked up her cup and took a sip of the soda to hide the flush on her face.

"What's this?" Bryce asked, looking suspiciously from Mark to Leslie and back.

"We bet on the figure-eight races. I lost," Mark said, taking a swig of his beer.

"You didn't bet against me, did you?" Bryce asked.

"I'm not that stupid. But I didn't mind losing." Mark tossed an M&M into his mouth, still studying Leslie.

This comment earned Leslie an intrigued look from Bryce.

Leslie rolled her eyes and folded her napkin into a tight square. She was supposed to be ignoring everything regarding Mark's love life. Why was she reminding herself of the flirtation of that evening and the kiss afterward? She shoved the memory back into the recesses of her mind.

"Mark doesn't normally like to lose," Bryce said, his gaze traveling between Mark and Leslie.

"Then why'd he pick the Patriots to lose?" Leslie asked. "Even I know they are favored to win, and I haven't a clue which color they are."

"Oh, they're the ones Tom Brady plays for," said Tara. "Reason enough to root for them, I'd say."

"Point him out to me," Leslie said. "I've got to see if he's worth the admiration."

"He won't be on the field for a while. The blue team has the ball now," Tara replied.

"If you're going to back the Patriots, you have to chip into the pot, too," Mark said.

"My vote all depends on Brady's derrière."

"I'd vote for that, too." Judi laughed.

"Hey!" Bryce yelled. "You're not supposed to be looking."

"Sorry, honey, but you have no butt." Judi walked over to Bryce and placed a quick kiss on his forehead. "At least if it's on TV, I can appreciate with my eyes and not with my hands."

Bryce looked only mildly appeased.

The blue team quickly turned the ball over, and Tom Brady was back on the field.

"There! There! Leslie, look!" Tara shouted.

Leslie studied the screen. "Which one is he?" '

"The one throwing the ball."

Leslie studied the television for a couple of plays. "This one?" She stood in front of the TV, pointing to one of the players. Bryce, Noah, and Mark yelled for her to move. "Not bad," Leslie conceded, laughing. "But I must say I've seen better." The image of Mark climbing down the ladder popped into her mind. Definitely better.

"Would anyone else like something to drink?" Leslie stopped at the refreshment table before returning to her seat. She poured herself another glass of soda and took a long drink. It stung every time Tara's hand landed on Mark's leg. Mark seemed to enjoy her attention, and from his seat he could probably see down her shirt to her navel.

It's what I chose, Leslie told herself. *At least he's happy*.

Judi placed another tray of cookies and a large bowl of popcorn on the table. "I think that's the last of the food that needs to come downstairs." She scooted a chair next to Leslie's. "Who's winning?"

"The Patriots must be. There's still only a dollar in the pot," Leslie said.

"Mark's going to get fleeced again." Judi scowled at Bryce. "I told you to be nice tonight."

"Mark was adamant the Patriots were going to fumble it this time. We couldn't convince him otherwise."

"I entered the bet of my own free will." Mark drew a cross over his heart with one finger.

Judi rolled her eyes. "They do this at every sporting event. It's as if they can't watch a game without money riding on it."

The game continued with good-natured ribbing and laughing and several contributions to the pot. People moved around and settled in different places. At halftime, Leslie found herself in the corner of the sectional next to Mark, with his arm resting on the back of the sofa behind her. Occasionally his fingertips brushed the back of her neck.

Leslie was having fun sharing in the inside jokes and talking about things besides work with Mark and Judi. Except for watching Tara drape herself all over Mark, Leslie felt as if she belonged here.

But she couldn't stay here. There weren't any jobs for her here.

She wished she could continue to enjoy these easy friendships with Mark and Judi and Bryce. Any position she took, she'd have to work her way up from the bottom again. Sure, Mr. Hanston would give her a good reference, but that wouldn't get her a junior partnership anywhere but with his firm. She would be working long days, courting clients. Each of her work relationships would be like her relationship with Chuck—tenuous and wondering when they were going to stab her in the back. She knew she didn't want to go back to that existence.

She dreaded the hours of grunt work. She wished she could finish her plans at the branch. But it was closing.

She sat up straighter as an idea occurred to her. She no longer worked for Boyd & Silverman, and they were selling the branch. The clients wouldn't go with them, and the noncompetition agreement didn't cover them. She could buy the branch and keep it open. Start her own company. Her nest egg should cover the cost of the building and any licenses she needed. Her severance package would keep her afloat for a few months if things were rocky.

Knotts Accounting. She liked the sound of that.

Mark caressed her earlobe and traced his finger along the edge of her ear. A shiver zipped down her spine. Everything felt right.

Chapter Twenty-two

L eslie pushed herself off the sofa when the panel of sportscasters came onto the screen to rehash the first half.

"Is everything all right?" Mark asked, grasping her hand.

"I need to make a couple of phone calls."

He raised an eyebrow but released her hand.

Leslie smiled and ran up the stairs into the quieter area of the kitchen.

When Leslie returned to the game, the betting jar was considerably fuller than when she'd left.

"Either Mark's wallet is empty, or the blue team scored," she said, taking a seat on the end of the sectional. Tara had scooted into Leslie's previous spot next to Mark.

"They got a field goal," Mark said. "They aren't winning, but they did score."

"We're getting his hopes up." Bryce grabbed a bowl of popcorn from the coffee table and cradled it in his lap.

"I thought you said he didn't like to lose," said Leslie, munching a cookie.

"I don't." Mark crossed his arms over his chest.

"But that doesn't mean he's not used to it," Bryce said. "It's not often that long shots pay off."

Mark dug his hand into Bryce's bowl of popcorn and chucked a handful at Bryce. Bryce scowled at him as he picked a kernel out of his collar.

"If I have to vacuum that sofa again, Mark . . ." Judi shook a finger at him.

"I'll clean up whatever Bryce doesn't eat."

Bryce chucked a handful of popcorn at Mark.

"Boys!" Judi scolded. She grabbed two handfuls of popcorn and whipped them at Bryce and Mark. "Stop. Throwing. Popcorn!"

Bryce threw a handful at her, scattering popcorn all over her and the floor. "I'm not throwing it. I'm spilling it accidentally in a strategic and planned manner. See?"

"Like this?" Judi threw another handful at the sofa, scattering kernels over all its occupants.

Soon popcorn was flying in all directions. Leslie ducked behind a sofa after throwing a handful herself into the melee but mostly at Tara. That tiny bit of revenge felt good. She'd never been in a food fight before and was more than a little shocked that she'd actually thrown popcorn.

She crouched with a pillow over her head, taking cover from the brunt of the assault. She heard Judi and Tara laughing. Mark, Bryce, and the other men yelled and made exploding sounds as popcorn flew from every direction.

A handful of kernels rained down on Leslie's head,

and she screamed as popcorn slipped down the front of her V-neck sweater.

A large body thumped down onto the floor beside her.

"Having fun?" Mark whispered, his face so close to hers, she could feel the warmth of his breath. Her heart pounded in her chest.

Before she could answer, Mark covered her body with his and pinned her to the floor. Popcorn pelted them. Bryce's laugh echoed over the sportscasters on the television. When the popcorn finally stopped falling, Mark rolled to his side, and Leslie looked up to see Bryce standing over them with an empty bowl, a wicked grin on his face.

Mark shook his head, sending popcorn flying. Bryce extended his hand, and Mark grasped it and pulled himself to his feet. He shook himself, dislodging the loose popcorn.

"Hey!" Leslie yelled, holding her hand in front of her face as the kernels tumbled down on her.

"Sorry!" He gave one last shake, then helped her up.

More popcorn slipped down her sweater. She rolled her shoulders and shook the front of her sweater. A few kernels fell out, but several stuck firmly in her bra.

Mark leaned closer and whispered in her ear, "Need some help?"

Warmth rushed through her. She glanced around the room.

"Later, then."

They spent the rest of the game laughing and picking popcorn out of the sofa cushions. When the game ended, the pot had a healthy amount of dollar bills and a handful of pennies Bryce had scrounged out of the sofa cushions. The Patriots lost the game in the last few seconds. Mark hefted the bowl of cash in triumph.

The party made their way upstairs, carrying empty trays and pop bottles. Tara stumbled on the last step. Mark managed to catch her before she landed face-first in the guacamole dip bowl.

Tara giggled. "Guess I had one beer too many." She pushed her hair back from her face.

"Maybe you shouldn't drive home," Bryce said.

Tara stumbled again. "I don't know where my keys are." She felt her pockets. "Can you give me a ride home, Mark? It's on your way."

Mark glanced at Leslie. "Sure. We'll leave your car here. You can pick it up tomorrow."

Tara laughed again and fell into Mark. He steadied her and ushered her out to his truck.

"I'd better go, too." Leslie said. "I have them blocked in." Leslie thanked Judi and followed Mark and Tara out. She jammed her key into the ignition and cranked the engine.

She tried not to watch Mark half drag Tara to the Suburban, but she couldn't tear her eyes away. He had the passenger door open and was trying to boost Tara into the seat. Tara had fallen against Mark, her arms draped around his neck.

Leslie took a deep breath and shifted into reverse. Tara hadn't drunk that much. She hadn't even finished the beer she'd started. Leslie drove the darkened streets to the bed-and-breakfast without meeting another car. She tried to ignore the edge of irritation biting at her stomach. She had no reason to be upset about Mark's taking Tara home. It was the nice thing to do. The responsible thing to do if Tara felt too inebriated to drive.

Leslie had no hold over Mark anyway.

Chapter Twenty-three

The next morning Leslie sprang out of bed, amazed at how different her outlook was today. Her dream was within reach. It wasn't the dream she had imagined for the last ten years, but it was the dream she wanted.

Leslie packed her business suit into a garment bag and hurried down the stairs. She popped the trunk of her car with the button on her key. She scraped the frost off the windshield, glad the predicted snowstorm had fizzled. Driving four hours in a snowstorm was not what she wanted this morning. She didn't expect smooth sailing, but she knew she was going to get what she wanted.

Her first stop in Chicago was the bank. As the clerk transferred the funds she needed and printed the check, Leslie called Tara with instructions for paperwork she'd need from the town offices and information to pass on to the customers.

She parked in her usual spot at what was now Boyd &

Silverman Accounting and pushed the trunk release. She'd dressed in jeans and a cashmere sweater for her drive. She grabbed her garment bag and briefcase and rode the parking garage elevator to the third floor. She hurried to the women's restroom and changed into her most severe black suit, wound her hair into a tight French twist, and slid her feet into three-inch black slingbacks.

Returning to the elevator, Leslie pressed the button for Boyd & Silverman's floor. She smoothed her hair after reviewing her reflection in the brushed stainless steel of the elevator door, then dropped her hand, remembering how Chuck had done the same thing. Chuck had no idea what was coming his way this morning.

She could have sent a representative, but she wanted to do this in person. She wanted to see Ms. Boyd squirm during the negotiations. Leslie knew she was offering the best deal Boyd & Silverman would see for the Carterville branch, and she knew they weren't going to like it.

The elevator door hissed open, and Leslie walked across the floor to Ms. Boyd's office. She asked Ms. Boyd's assistant, a muscled blond, to announce her.

The receptionist pressed a button on the intercom and then waved Leslie into the office.

Leslie strode into Ms. Boyd's office. She hadn't wasted any time redecorating and moving into the larger corner office. The classic walnut furniture had been replaced with a glass-topped desk and chairs from the set of *The Jetsons*.

Ms. Boyd stood behind her desk as Leslie entered. Chuck lounged on the edge of her desk. He stood quickly and buttoned his suit jacket. He nodded to her and walked stiffly around the desk and dropped into a chair.

"Ms. Knotts," Ms. Boyd said. "It's a surprise to see you. Chuck was telling me what he thought we could sell the property for and steps that have been made toward advertising it."

Sure, he was. "Wonderful." She smiled. "Then you'll be in the proper frame of mind for our meeting," Leslie said.

"Sit." Ms. Boyd gestured to the seat on Chuck's left.

Leslie met her gaze, then perched on the edge of the chair and snapped the locks open on her briefcase. She kept her movements slow and careful. She would not let Ms. Boyd rattle her. She withdrew a neat stack of papers.

"Ms. Knotts," Ms. Boyd said, sitting in her chair and rolling it closer to her desk. She placed her elbows on the translucent surface and pressed her fingertips together. "We have no desire to continue a business relationship with you at this time. The severance package we offered is more than generous, and we're not willing to renegotiate."

Leslie glanced at Chuck. A smirk tugged his lips. If he expected her to grovel, demand more money in severance or beg for her job back, he had a surprise coming. She couldn't wait to sever any connection with him and his company.

"I have no desire to have an ongoing relationship with Boyd and Silverman Accounting. Nor do I wish to renegotiate anything." She kept her tone clipped but neutral.

She'd been jerked around enough by these two in the last month. She wasn't going to allow them to intimidate or anger her. It may have been personal to them, but she could keep this all business.

"I'm afraid I don't understand the nature of your visit," Ms. Boyd said with an irritated look.

Leslie returned her gaze unflinchingly. "I am presenting a purchase offer for the Carterville branch. The company I represent wishes to take immediate possession." Leslie placed a stack of papers on the desktop. She'd stayed up until two the previous night writing the contract. It was a basic sales agreement, but she'd reviewed it several times to ensure all the details were correct.

Chuck's jaw dropped. He quickly closed it and sat straighter in his seat. "You're doing this for Hanston, aren't you? According to the agreement you signed, you can't have any contact with his company for at least a year." Chuck's face was turning red.

Leslie narrowed her gaze on Chuck. He was too upset about this. Hanston must be snatching up branches and their clients, and that had Ms. Boyd and Chuck scared. She allowed the ends of her lips to curve.

"There was nothing in the noncompetition agreement saying I couldn't present an offer for the sale. It only specified I could not work as an accountant for companies considered direct competition. You gave me a specific list."

Chuck grimaced.

Leslie guessed making the noncompetition agreement too specific was an oversight. He'd wanted to ruin her career.

Ms. Boyd flipped through the pages, scanning the terms of the offer. She arrived on the last page, where Leslie had included some very specific obligations on the part of Boyd & Silverman Accounting. Her favorite was removing the old customer files. She'd dealt with enough of it; they could dispose of the rest.

"No. We won't accept." Ms. Boyd slapped the top pages and shoved the papers across the desk. The top one floated off the pile and slipped to the floor.

"It's the best offer you'll receive." Leslie forced herself to keep her cool. No wonder all the prestigious clients were leaving for Hanston & Associates. Who wanted to work with irrationality? Ms. Boyd had refused the offer before she considered whether this would be good for her company or not.

Leslie felt a momentary sympathy for Chuck. He was a partner in this firm, and it was going to collapse before he got his new business cards printed. But Chuck had made his choice.

Leslie wanted the branch, and she would get it. Even if it meant spelling it out for them.

"I think you should reconsider. It's a fair offer." She picked up the paper from the floor and placed it back on Ms. Boyd's desk. She pushed the stack back toward the scowling partner.

"We said no," Chuck said, reaching for the stack of papers.

Leslie turned to Chuck, barely hiding her annoyance. "This isn't any of your business, is it? In fact, I don't think you are even involved in this negotiation." She turned back to Ms. Boyd, waiting for her response.

"Chuck is correct. I've already turned down your offer. Why are you still here?" Ms. Boyd sniffed, her nostrils tightening as if she smelled sour milk.

Leslie stiffened her shoulders. She wouldn't be ruffled by their attempts to bully her. "If I were in a similar situation, I might agree with your philosophy. However, knowing what I do about this property and the current state of Boyd and Silverman Accounting, I believe you will accept my offer."

Ms. Boyd's eyes narrowed on her. Leslie met her gaze without flinching. Ms. Boyd wasn't going to intimidate her. They were both CEOs now, equals, but Leslie knew more about the real estate market of Carterville than Ms. Boyd did. If Boyd's clients were leaving as quickly as it sounded, they should be desperate to consolidate the business and increase their cash assets.

"Why would I do that?" Ms. Boyd leaned back in her chair and toyed with the stylus of her personal organizer.

"Several reasons, Ms. Boyd. First, Boyd and Silverman Accounting is in financial trouble. Circumstances are shifting too quickly to be sure what cash flow you will have in a year, let alone six months. You aren't sure how bad things are yet or how many clients are going to pull out. You need to tighten your hold on what you do have and eliminate loose ends. Selling the branch would eliminate one headache and one loose end. As you well know, this time of year is the bread and butter of the accounting industry. You can't bleed clients now and stay afloat. The customers in Carterville have no loyalty to you. Letting them go would be painless to your operations and would allow you to focus on your remaining clients."

The stylus froze. Rusted wheels ground in Ms. Boyd's head. Leslie caught an almost imperceptible nod.

"Second, the real estate market in Carterville is depressed. Homes sit on the market an average of twenty-four months, and commercial property can sit vacant for years. Holding the property will not increase the possibility of a higher offer. In fact, the offers—if there are any—will only get lower. Selling now ensures the best selling price."

"This offer is well below the advertised price." Ms. Boyd lifted the advertisement off her desk and waved it at her.

"The amount offered is exactly the amount of the appraisal," Leslie replied. "I have a copy of it here, if you haven't seen it." She glanced at Chuck. "I was not consulted about the advertisement."

Chuck squirmed uncomfortably in his seat.

Ms. Boyd nodded, and Leslie retrieved a copy from her briefcase and passed it across Ms. Boyd's desk. After flipping through a couple pages, Ms. Boyd scowled at Chuck. "You advertised four times more than its current market value."

Chuck simply shrugged. Leslie knew he couldn't defend his decision. He'd selected the number at random without any research.

"But they want all the equipment, too," Chuck exclaimed, pointing to one of the stipulations. "Most of it is brand-new."

"It would cost you more to have the equipment moved to another office than to include it in the sale. Including the office equipment would be the least compensation you could offer for the inconvenience of storing thirty years of paperwork until you remove it."

"Until I see some credit history or investor information, I can't accept your offer." Ms. Boyd shook her head.

Leslie was sure Ms. Boyd would sign the papers. She reached for her briefcase and extracted an envelope.

"How do I know the buyer can actually pay the amount offered? I can't afford to have this offer fall through. I would have to ask for a sizeable down payment as security."

Leslie suppressed a grin. "I should have a deposit in my checking account for approximately forty percent drawn on the accounts of Boyd and Silverman Accounting. Are you concerned with the validity of their funds?"

Ms. Boyd's face turned slightly purple.

Chuck opened and closed his mouth as he put the pieces together. "You're buying the branch? And staying with the redneck clients?" He snorted.

"As a matter of fact, yes. As I told you before, I have a promising tax return season starting and have been courting several business clients. I am completely capable of fulfilling my end of the offer." She gazed steadily at Ms. Boyd, waiting for her to crack.

Ms. Boyd cleared her throat. "Let me see that offer again." She reached across the desk and grabbed the papers from Chuck. She flipped through the pages quickly, initially items as needed. "We agree to your offer as written." She scrawled her signature across the bottom of the final page and handed her the papers.

Leslie added her own signature. She opened the envelope and held up the cashier's check. "Here is the full amount."

Ms. Boyd reached for the check, but Leslie pulled it away and tucked it back into its envelope. "My representative will deliver it at closing."

Leslie dropped the check and the signed agreement into her briefcase. She walked to the door and opened it. She nodded at Chuck and Ms. Boyd as she left, wondering how many flies would land in their mouths before they remembered to close them.

Chapter Twenty-four

Leslie returned to Carterville that afternoon elated. She went straight to her office. *Her office*. She smiled. She liked the sound of that. She had tax return appointments scheduled for the next month, and most people were only getting their W-2s that week. This tax season was going to be quite profitable. She just had to work on business clients, and she'd have steady customers all year round. Putting Ms. Boyd and Chuck the slimeball in their places hadn't hurt her mood either.

She signed the incorporation forms Tara had picked up and shoved them into her briefcase. She'd drop them off on her way back to the Lilac Bower. She thought of it as home, but she'd have to find a more permanent place to live now. She waved good-bye to Tara, who was still answering calls, and headed for her car.

Mark was waiting in the parking lot, leaning against his Suburban.

Leslie steeled herself against the wave of attraction that washed over her. He exuded relaxation. One word, one gesture, and Leslie would forget their charade was over and that he had moved on to Tara. Leslie waved to him and fumbled with her keys. She couldn't let herself succumb to these feelings. She pushed the unlock button, and her door locks popped free.

"Tara should be out shortly. Glad to see you got your truck fixed," she called to Mark, feeling happy enough to risk small talk with him. "I forgot to ask what was wrong with it."

"Out of gas." He laughed and shook his head. He pushed himself away from the vehicle and strode over to her. He leaned against the rear door of her car and crossed his arms over his chest. He laughed half to himself.

"You ran out of gas?" Leslie looked at him skeptically. She opened her car door and tossed her briefcase onto the passenger seat. Stuffing her arms into the sleeves of her coat, she said, "You know, most cars have this gauge right in the dashboard that tells you how full the gas tank is. Mine even has a warning light for when the tank gets too low."

"The gauge's been broken since Bryce owned it. I use the odometer to tell me how far I've driven and when I need a fill-up. But my odometer said I should have half a tank left."

"What happened, then?"

"I think Bryce's mom stuck a hose into the tank and siphoned the gas out."

"Would she do that?" Leslie rested her hands on her

open car door. Mark grinned as if he found the situation hilarious. It sounded like a cruel practical joke to her.

"Dinah is Bryce's mom," he reminded her.

"Right. I'd forgotten." Leslie finally understood. The Library Ladies' schemes. "They are persistent. And creative. Who was supposed to pick you up?"

"You." He stared at her with such intensity, her cheeks burned.

"But . . . but . . ." she stammered. Couldn't they see he wanted Tara? "You could have called Tara. I bet she'd have been there in a flash." Leslie glanced through the office window. Tara chatted happily on the phone.

"I did."

Leslie winced inwardly. He'd called Tara to rescue him before he called her. He'd probably danced around his kitchen after she told him they could end the charade.

"Tara claimed she couldn't get away. Phones were too busy." His voice was low and husky. "She suggested I try you."

Oh. And she'd run right out the door. Leslie's heart pounded in her chest. How desperate did that look?

She'd finally gotten her career corrected, but this thing with Mark wouldn't go away. She'd fallen in love with him, but he didn't return her feelings. He never would. She'd told him they could end the charade. He wasn't forced to hang around her anymore.

But they still seemed to run into each other a lot. Sure, it was a small town, and she couldn't avoid him. At the Super Bowl party, he'd hinted at something more. Then he left with Tara.

Now he was here again. Couldn't he leave well enough alone? Leslie couldn't deny she wanted him to be around. As long as he wasn't drooling over Tara. He had become a great friend, but she wanted more, and that scared her so much, she pretended those feelings didn't exist.

Leslie didn't know where to look. Mark stared at her, and she forced herself not to fidget. She could overcome this. Follow her professional instincts. Stick to business, she told herself. You're safe there.

"Your final check for the project will be ready tomorrow morning. I'll leave it with Tara if you want to pick it up." Leslie climbed into her car and pulled the door shut. She finger-waved in what she hoped was a nonchalant manner to Mark and left. She glanced into the mirror as she pulled out of the parking lot. Mark stood in her empty parking spot, facing her instead of the office.

What was wrong with him? she thought as she accelerated down the street. She was trying to make this as easy as possible. Every time she saw him, she became more confused.

That evening, Leslie stacked her laundry in her basket and carried it down to the washing machine in the basement. On the way back upstairs, she found Minnie in the back sitting room with her feet propped on a flowered ottoman and the television muted in front of her.

Leslie glanced at the show. A purple-haired woman displayed a masquerade-masked porcelain cat. It looked like an infomercial, but Leslie doubted that the cat had any amazing cleaning abilities. Closed-captioning scrolled across the bottom.

Minnie greeted her and went back to scowling at the television. "Gonna have to get a new television. The sound is broke on this one. I cranked the volume all the way up, and nothing changes. It's got this typing on the screen, but I can't see the prices of the items or the number to call." She thumped the remote down on the arm of her chair. "I thought TVs were supposed to last longer than this. It's only a year old. They just don't make stuff like they used to."

Leslie glanced at the screen. MUTE flashed in an upper corner.

"May I see the remote?" Leslie asked.

Minnie handed it to her. "Every channel's the same."

Leslie found the mute button and pressed it. The salesperson's voice shouted that the porcelain cats were available for a limited time only. Leslie quickly thumbed the volume button, returning the sound to a more pleasing level.

"How'd you do that?" Minnie asked, gaping. "It's been that way for a week."

Leslie showed her the mute button.

"Can you get those dumb words off the screen, too? I can't stand them."

Leslie navigated through the on-screen menu, and soon the closed-captioning blinked off.

Minnie sighed in relief. "That's so much better. Now I can call and place an order. The number flashed on the screen, and Minnie scribbled it down on a notepad.

"How'd things go today?" Minnie asked as she punched the number into her phone.

"Busy, but everything worked out. The branch is mine. You want to watch a movie?"

"Find something." Minnie tossed the remote to her. Leslie scrolled through the channels. When she finished, Minnie was on the phone with the sales representative.

"They put me on hold." Minnie pushed the speakerphone button and dropped the phone into her lap. Scratchy elevator music echoed over the handset.

"Anything on?"

"No."

The hold music stopped on the phone, and an operator's voice called, "Home Shopping Network. How may I help you? Is anyone there?"

Minnie scrambled for the phone and placed it to her ear. She told the operator she wanted to order one of the porcelain cats advertised on the show.

"Well, thank you anyway." Minnie pushed a button on the phone and dropped it onto the end table with a flourish. "Don't that beat all! They sold out. All the cats are gone. Even the ugly one with the fangs." She stared at the television for a moment. "I'm so glad you're staying in town. Carterville needs more young professionals. The Ladies had a feeling about you. We knew you'd stay around."

"You know, I never considered any deviation from the career path I chose in high school. I had all the steps planned out. I never thought about other ways to reach my goals until I moved here. I can't wait to meet my first customer. I can't believe how hard you and the other Library Ladies worked to get people interested. The branch never had this many appointments."

"We've got some connections." Minnie nodded. "That happens in a small town. You get to know people. Their wants and desires. Even when they don't know themselves. Some people need a little push to take a chance on what they want. That's how it was with Mark. I could tell he hated the job at the school, but he wouldn't listen to me. Bryce had to bully him to quit and start out on his own. Once he knew what he wanted, it didn't take much to get him going. I think you're the same way. When did you decide to buy the branch? Yesterday?"

Leslie nodded. "It all worked out, and now I have everything I want." *Everything I can have,* she added to herself.

"Do you?" Minnie straightened the phone on the end table. "I think there's something or someone more out there for you."

"Someone?" Leslie choked.

"If Mark is what you want, you should go after him."

"What . . . what if he doesn't want me?"

She didn't realize she'd said it out loud until Minnie said, "You'll never know unless you ask."

Chapter Twenty-five

Leslie threw the car into park, breathing deeply. Minnie's apple pie was on the seat next to her and smelled cinnamony. She pulled her keys out and dropped them onto the center console.

Minnie had shooed her out the door so fast, Leslie had barely been able to switch her slippers for boots and grab her coat. She wanted to get everything out in the open between her and Mark. At least then they'd know where they stood with each other.

She'd managed to snatch the envelope holding Mark's tax information before Minnie shut the door behind her. She could use it as an excuse for her visit if Tara opened the door wearing nothing but Mark's T-shirt.

Leslie debated whether she wanted to do this. She'd made the decision instantly when talking with Minnie. But when she faced knocking on his door, all her doubts rushed back. This wasn't like walking into Boyd & Silverman and

255

purchasing the Carterville branch. It wasn't like starting her own business either. In those cases, she'd risked only money and her career—things she could work hard for and get back. If Mark turned her down, she didn't know if her heart would ever be whole again.

She looked out her car window at his house blazing with light. She had come this far; she would go the last few steps.

That's what a CEO would do. They took the risks for potential success. Now that she was a CEO, she could do the same.

Leslie tucked the envelope of tax information under her arm, picked up the pie with one hand, and opened the car door with other. Her heart thumped in her chest as she climbed the porch stairs. She pressed the doorbell and heard its quiet melody inside the house.

The high-pitched screech of a saw answered from the upstairs. Mark hadn't heard the doorbell. She pushed the door open and stepped inside.

"Mark?" she called, closing the door behind her.

She was answered by another buzz of the saw.

Leslie followed the noise to the stairway. She called again in the quiet when she heard the saw wind down.

"I'm upstairs. Just a minute," he called.

She climbed the stairs to a wide-open floor. Several piles of wood littered the floor. The tangy scent of cedar floated in the air.

Mark stood with his back to her over a piece of wood supported by two sawhorses. He was scribbling on the wood with the nub of a pencil.

He was shirtless.

Leslie's body refused to take in oxygen. Sawdust clung to the glistening muscles of his back and arms. His usual jeans and tool belt were slung around his hips. The waist of his jeans hung low enough to reveal an inch of red boxer shorts.

Just seeing him made her happy. Tension eased out of her and was replaced by the blush of love.

Definitely worth the risk.

He bent to pick up the saw at his feet. Somehow Leslie managed to find enough oxygen to speak, but she wasn't sure what to say. Should she blurt out what she wanted? Why hadn't she prepared what she wanted to say?

Because the short drive here hadn't given her time.

She scrambled for words. He turned to face her, giving her a full view of the ridged muscles of his abdomen. He chucked his pencil onto the pile of wood, and her eyes finally reached his face.

"What brings you here?"

Sawdust littered his hair and eyebrows. A smear of pinkish paint crossed the thigh of his jeans. She took a deep breath, drawing in the scent of cedar and soap.

"Minnie asked me to bring this pie over," she said, wondering if he could hear the pounding of her heart. She gestured lamely with the pie. That wasn't what she wanted to say.

She wanted Mark. She loved him. Three simple words. Why was it so hard?

Mark stared down into her eyes. He took the pie and set it on a pile of wood. It wobbled on the uneven surface. Leslie stepped closer and pushed it to a more secure location.

Her movement brought her within a hairs breadth of Mark's chest. Her knees shook, and he steadied her with a hand on her arm.

It was now or never. She had to tell him. It didn't matter what he said. She just had to say it.

"Minnie didn't ask me to come here," Leslie said, licking her lips and looking up at him. "I told her I was coming, and she sent the pie."

"What'd you need?" He dropped his hand and hooked his thumbs in his belt loops.

Leslie regretted her wool sweater. The loft was eight hundred degrees. Or maybe that was the man standing in front of her.

"I wanted to drop off your tax information." She waved the manila envelope in her other hand.

"Thanks." Mark took the envelope and studied its clasp, bending the metal tabs back and forth. "I could've picked it up at the office or at Minnie's. You didn't need to come all the way out here. How bad's the damage?"

Leslie winced inwardly and inched toward the door. "You only owe a hundred bucks. I've got a disk in there, too. You can upload it to the computer and . . ."

Her gaze met Mark's and locked. She stopped her retreat. She wasn't going to leave without knowing. A CEO didn't run from a confrontation. "But that's not what I came here to say either." She studied his face. "I'm not leaving Carterville," she blurted. "I've found a job here. I'm going to be here for a while."

"What happened to corporate America and Fortune 500 companies?" He tossed the envelope next to the pie.

"This position fits me better, and I can make a difference to people who are special to me." Her voice sounded much calmer than her hammering pulse should have allowed. She forced herself to maintain eye contact. The muscles around his eyes seemed to relax, but that could have been her imagination.

"Who will you be working for?" he asked.

"I'm starting my own business, Knotts Accounting and Tax Service. I bought the branch. I decided to cut some rungs out of the corporate ladder. I'm not going to depend on someone else to get me to the top of a Fortune 500 company. I'm going to build my own empire."

"Congratulations!" Mark threw his arms around her. He hugged her tightly and swung her around the room. She relished the feel of his arms around her. His strength and support encouraged her. She wanted to relax into his body and find the comfort she had found there before.

"Edith will be happy about the sale. She'll want to find you a house now." He grinned. "I'm so excited for you. You know, the Ladies will be relentless. We'll have to renew the charade or have a nasty breakup."

Leslie hesitated. "I hadn't thought about that." She glanced at the uncovered window. She thought she saw a car park across the street. Tara. It had to be. Who else would come by his place at this time of night? Besides herself, that is. This was ridiculous. She should leave. Cut her losses. He didn't need to know she'd come to give him her heart. But then she'd never know how he felt.

If she was going to go after what she wanted, she had to start now.

"Are you expecting someone?" she asked. If he said yes, she'd have her answer, and she could leave.

"No, why?" Mark followed her gaze to the window.

"I thought I saw someone park across the street."

"They weren't coming to see me." Mark shrugged, turning away from the window, his hands on his hips.

"Is there someplace we can sit down? I need to tell you a Library Lady story."

Mark grasped her hand and tugged her over to a pile of two-by-fours. He wiped away the sawdust and sat. Leslie perched beside him but sprang back up. She couldn't think clearly enough with that much of her body in contact with his.

Leslie paced in front of him. "I've been set up before, too, you know." She stared out the darkened window. "I met this group of women who thought their sole purpose in life was to bring people together, and they were very good at it.

"They saw a lonely career woman and decided she needed someone. The person they chose for her was sick of their schemes and enlisted my help in outsmarting them. That worked okay until something went wrong." She took a deep breath, preparing for the little words that screeched to a halt at the end of her tongue.

"A busty blond showed up and ruined everything?" Mark joked.

She whispered. "No. I forgot it was a charade, and I fell in love with him."

Mark stared at her, the look in his eyes stunned. He started to say something but stopped, his mouth open.

Uh-oh, she thought, time to backpedal. She spoke quickly. "I realize you are probably shocked by this. I've been off balance since I realized what I felt. But I've decided to take some risks, and I had to tell you how I felt. I know you've said Tara is your ideal woman, but . . ." She trailed off. He obviously didn't reciprocate her feelings. Well, at least she'd spoken. And that was all she needed to do, right?

CEOs got rejected all the time. Deals went sour. Risks got too big. A CEO shrugged it off and went to work the next day.

Then why did she feel as if there was a jagged hole where her heart had been?

Mark took a deep breath, and Leslie's gaze slid to his expanding chest. The sawdust there begged her to dust it off. Mark lifted her hand to his lips and kissed the back of it. Then he turned her hand over and placed a kiss in her open palm. He closed her fingers over the place where his lips had been and tilted her face toward his.

"I never said Tara was my ideal woman. Tara's only ever been a friend. I admitted I was attracted to blonds with large breasts," he said carefully.

"What's the difference?" She pulled away from him, wishing he would release her hand and hoping the cessation of contact would stem the heat traveling through her body.

"Strong, attractive women have always drawn my attention, but I never knew why it didn't last until I saw your brand of confidence and determination," Mark said. He spoke slowly, as if finding the right words was as difficult for him as it had been for her. He pushed a loose tendril of hair behind her ear. "You were the whole package. Beautiful, fun, and smart. Leslie, our relation-ship stopped being a charade a long time ago for me. I wanted to tell you, but I knew you were leaving town. I guess I should've said something sooner. But I'm telling you now." He paused, looking down at their hands. "I've fallen in love with you, too."

Leslie's eyes started to sting. She wouldn't give in to the tears. *CEOs don't cry.* She brushed her hand against her eyes, but the salty water smeared across her cheeks.

Mark gave her a kiss that seemed to last an eternity. His lips trailed down her neck to her ear, and he whispered, "Minnie will be insufferable. Her scheme worked."

Minnie passed the binoculars to Edith. "See? I told you it would work," she said, pointing to Mark's window.

Edith removed her glasses and propped the binoculars against her nose. She peered out the side window of the parked car. "We're still at one hundred percent."

Dinah grabbed the binoculars from the backseat. "We never fail."

"Let me look." Yvonne squinted through the binocu-lars. "I can barely see a thing. The windows are steamed up, but I guess that proves it. One hundred percent."

They all stared up at the figures of Mark and Leslie silhouetted against the window.

"Perhaps we should give them some privacy," Edith said, reaching for the keys in the ignition. "Let's cele-brate with some punch."

"They can't see us anyway." Minnie slapped her hand

away and grabbed for the binoculars again. "Next time we need to check for confirmation, we take Yvonne's mini-van. There are just too many of us in here. Who should we work on next?" she asked, focusing the glasses.

"I'm available!" Tara piped up.